Sexy Greek Go(

Austin Kalin

Inkitt

Chapter 1: Mine

Sam

"Time out!" The umpire yelled.

I got up and ran to my best friend Kyrn who was at the pitcher's mound.

"Okay Kyrn. You got this. The count is three-two. There are two outs so far with a runner on third base. All we need is one more strike and we win the championships!" I said trying to encourage her.

She nodded her head and gave me a nervous smile. "Thanks."

I smiled at her brightly in reassurance. "Anytime."

I ran to the plate and crouched waiting for her pitch. I looked at my coach and he gave me the sign for an inside ball. I quickly repeated the sign for Kyrn, and she nodded. She pitched it and the batter ticked it, causing it to shoot straight up in the air. I threw my catcher's helmet off and ran over to where Kyrn was.

"Mine!" Kyrn yelled. The first baseman and I went to her sides just in case she missed it.

She caught the ball, and everyone jumped up cheering.

"We won!" I yelled as I jumped on Kyrn. She laughed and tried to balance herself so we both didn't fall over in the sand.

"Northwestern High wins the championship! Northwestern High Wild Cats are your new 2013 softball champions!" The announcer shouted excitedly.

The team ran out to the middle of the diamond and jumped on one another—screaming and shouting, praising one another on doing a good job throughout the softball season.

"Captains, would you like to do the honors?" One of our teammates asked, handing us the Gatorade jug. Kyrn and I looked at each other and smiled.

"Yes please," I said taking it.

Kyrn and I walked to the coach and dumped it on him. We busted out laughing while he jumped around.

Once he saw Kyrn and I laughing, he calmed down and smiled while shaking his head. "I'm really going to miss you two girls."

"Don't worry. I'm so coming back next season and helping you coach," I said with a big smile.

"Me too. Duh!" Kyrn said.

"Good," our coach said, pulling us into hugs.

Kyrn and I both shrieked as our jerseys became soaked with blue Gatorade.

"Sam, Dad and I are leaving now for Italy. Okay?" my mom said as she walked over to us.

"Same here, Kyrn. Now remember we left our debit card at Sam's house along with your clothes. We will be back in two months. Behave, you two," Kyrn's mom said smiling.

"We will mother," Kyrn said with a smile.

Kyrn and I get to have my house for two months by ourselves. I know a lot of you are wondering that it's kind of stupid to leave two eighteen-year-old girls alone for two months. But my parents think it will teach us responsibility, since we'll be in college next year. They want us to see what it's like living by ourselves. Kyrn and I haven't decided if we wanted to buy an apartment, or still live at home when we go to college. But my parents said by doing this, it will help us choose.

Kyrn and I giggled as we mocked our parents' lectures about how we need to behave and not talk to strangers. You know, the stuff your parents tell you a million times a day. Or at least ten times before you walk out the door to go hang out with friends.

My mom lightly smacked the back of my head when we got to the car. "I saw that."

"Bye Mom, bye Dad. Love you guys," I said, giving them both hugs and kisses with a sly smile.

"Remember, call us every day," my mom said sternly before getting in the car.

I nodded just to satisfy her. I knew she was serious and would probably come back and hunt me down if I didn't tell her what I was doing every moment of the day. Don't get me wrong, I love my mom, but she is so strict. But I know she's like that because she loves me, and I wouldn't have it any other way.

Kyrn and I waved until our parents were gone before we both started screaming in excitement.

"I think a shopping trip is in need sometime this week. I mean like, seriously, we both have debit cards now," I pulled mine out of my wallet.

"I know. But you better hurry and go take a shower if you want to surprise Brett for your two-year anniversary." She smiled.

"Oh shit. I'm going to be late!" I cussed as I checked my phone. I couldn't be late for this. I had a huge surprise for him and I didn't want to mess this up!

We ran to my car and jumped in.

"What did you get him?" she asked as she buckled up and I put the car in drive.

"He loves getting his picture taken with me, so I got him a picture frame with his favorite picture of us in it, and tickets to see the Green Bay Packers. I don't know why he likes the Packers. I'm more of a Vikings fan myself," I said teasingly.

"You and football…" She shook her head at me as she rested her elbow on the window.

"What? You like the Steelers!" I retorted.

"This is true." She laughed in defeat.

The car ride home consisted of us trying to out-do each other about listing off some of our favorite teams' highlights. We finally made it to her house where I dropped Kyrn off and went home.

After getting ready, which didn't take very long, I hopped back in my car. I arrived at Brett's house in ten minutes, and quickly made sure I looked presentable before unbuckling my seatbelt and making my way to the front door.

'Is he home?' I thought.

I called out, but no one responded.

"Hmm," I hummed, as I closed the door and walked into his living room.

I heard some noise upstairs which made me smile in excitement as I ran up the stairs with his present in my hands. I couldn't wait to give it to him! I tiptoed over to his door, and quietly opened it and walked in. I wanted this to be a surprise.

And oh boy. Was I right? What I saw next was a surprise.

"Hey Brett, I got—oh my gosh," I said, the last part in a whisper.

A very naked Brett, was on top of a very naked Tasha, and they were all up in each other's grill.

"I love you, Tasha," he said, leaning down and kissing her.

I cleared my throat.

He quickly looked up. When his eyes landed on me, with my arms crossed, they widened. "Oh my gosh. Sam baby, when did you get here?" he asked quickly as he got off Tasha.

"Hey Sam, I was just uh—" Tasha started.

I cut her off "Shut up." I said as she quickly looked down and wrapped the sheets around herself tighter.

I look at the picture and grabbed the tickets off the picture frame, before I threw it on the ground.

Tasha gasped and shielded her eyes as glass flew across the room.

"Happy two-year-anniversary, *boyfriend*," I spat as he looked at me with so much regret. I held both football tickets and ripped them in his face. His eyes widened. "Go to hell," I said, before I ran out of there.

I heard his footsteps following me as I rushed to my car and locked it, with him banging on my windows.

"Sam!" he cried as he held the sheets around his waist tighter so they wouldn't fall down. "Sam please! Let me explain."

I ignored him and turned my car on while putting it in reverse. I hit the gas pedal and watched as Brett jumped back so he didn't get run over.

Once I got to the street, I grabbed my phone and dialed Kyrn's number.

"Hello?" she asked.

"Kyrn," I sobbed.

"Oh sweetie, what happened?"

"He's a lying, sex-craved man-whore!" I yelled.

"Okay. I'm on my way, need anything?"

"Movies and ice cream please," I cried harder.

"Okay hun, I'll be right over."

"Okay. Thank you. Bye."

"Anytime. Bye."

I put my phone down with a groan as the light turned red. I flipped through the radio and stopped once I heard Hollywood Undead playing. I cranked up the music to see if I could forget everything I'd just seen.

I opened my eyes and looked up to see a giant, red F350 truck pull up next to me.

'Hot damn,' I whispered to myself. I loved trucks. It was a weakness of mine.

But what really got me were the four guys inside. They were all extremely attractive. Then there was me, red puffy eyes and tears running down my face.

But the guy that really stuck out was the one driving. He had black spiked hair and grey eyes. He was in the middle of talking when he looked at me.

His friends tried to get his attention, but all he could do was smile. He looked like he had just won the lottery, but all of a sudden he got angry. Probably thinking I was some creep staring at him. His eyes turned dark, and they almost looked…black.

I was starting to get freaked out, and I quickly looked at the red light wishing it was green already.

The Lord seemed to have answered my prayers, because the light suddenly turned green and I stepped on the gas. After getting the hell out of there and arriving at my house, I changed into my p.js and waited for Kyrn to show up.

It didn't take long before I heard knocking on my door.

"Hey," Kyrn said as I let her in. She was wearing an oversized sweatshirt, baggy sweatpants, and had her hair in a messy bun.

So, she pretty much looked like me, except with the puffy face and the tears streaming down her face.

She handed me my tub of mint chocolate-chip ice cream and put in the Last Song.

I told her everything. Then it got a lot more emotional because it reminded her of her last boyfriend Trey. He did the same thing, also with Tasha. She was Northwestern High's slut.

So here we were, crying our eyes out, eating tubs and tubs of ice cream, and watching sad romantic movies. Probably not a good choice, but we didn't really care at the moment. I mean—can you blame us? I think not.

We were at the part where her dad dies, when a knock on the door interrupted us. I groaned in frustration and got up, while wiping away all of my tears.

I opened the door and started yelling. "Listen. My friend and I are not in the mood, so if you could please leave that would be nice." I spoke without looking at whoever was there, and continued to watch the movie.

Bad idea.

"Mine," I heard someone growl softly. And yes, I did say growl.

"What?" I turn around and my eyes went huge.

It was the same group of guys that had seen me crying in my car at the stoplight. I took time to look at him. He had a white, tight fitting shirt so I could see his muscles, dark blue faded jeans scrunched at the bottom because of his combat boots.

His other friends were tall just like him. The one on the left had short brown hair and blue eyes, the one of the right had shaggy dirty blond hair and green eyes, and the other one next to him had shaggy brown hair and brown eyes.

6

I was pulled out of my thoughts when the black haired guy pulled me into his chest. He put his face in the crook of my neck and breathed in deeply.

I felt my body tense as he grabbed my hand and glided his thumb across my knuckles in a loving manner.

"Okay. This is a little too weird for me. So if you could let me go, that would be great," I said pushing him away. Well, I should say, trying to push him away because he didn't move an inch. He growled again and pulled me even closer to him. "Mine."

I looked up and noticed the short brown-haired guy smiling like crazy.

Uh, yeah. Because this isn't weird at all.

Sam! Now is not the time to be sarcastic. Save that for another time. Preferably a less dangerous time.

"What's taking you so long, Sam?" Kyrn asked walking outside to where I was.

"Mine," the brown-haired guy said. And with that he pulled Kyrn into his chest.

"Congrats, dude," the other men said to him.

"You too," he said to the black-haired guy, and then smiled down at Kyrn.

Kyrn and I looked at each other warily.

"Can you please let us go?" she asked.

Both guys looked at us and growled softly.

"No," they said in unison.

"Fine. Shall we?" I asked Kyrn.

She smirked evilly at me. "We shall."

We kneed them in the crotch. When they fell, Kyrn and I quickly ran into the house and locked the door.

About three seconds later there was banging.

"Leave us alone, you bastards!" Kyrn yelled.

"Seriously. Go away!" I yelled at them.

The banging on the door only got louder.

"Back door?" I asked her. Kyrn nodded, and we ran out the back door and slipped into the shadows. Thank God it was dark outside.

"What the hell do they want?" she whispered.

"How should I know?" I whispered, looking at her. "I've never met them before."

As if they'd heard us, they turned toward us.

"Shit!" we screamed and started to run.

About five seconds later, I heard a yelp.

I looked to my right and saw the short brown-haired guy picking up Kyrn..

"Let her go!" I screamed and ran toward him. But before I could even take a step, the black haired guy picked me up..

"Kyrn!" I screamed.

"Sam!" She screamed back.

Our eyes widened and realization hit us like a train. We realized we were being kidnapped by Sexy Greek God kidnappers.

Chapter 2: Chloroform and Car Chases

Xavier

"Is this the house?" Jay asked me as we walked up to the front porch.

"Yep. Her scent leads straight to here." I looked over the front of the house.

It had a nice, warm cozy feeling to it. It was a three-story grayish-blue colonial. There was a brightly flowering garden in the front lawn leading up the sidewalk. I'm pretty sure if my mom was here, she would be banging on the door asking my mate's mom how she got her garden the way it was. My mom had such a green thumb, but this layout would be something she would definitely be jealous about.

But back to the most important thing. My mate. My wolf and I are still upset. Seeing our lovely mate cry like that, we wanted to know why she was crying.

When she pulled up next to my truck and we locked eyes, I knew she was my mate and I couldn't be any happier. But when I looked more closely at her, her eyes were all red and puffy and she had tears streaming down her face. I wanted to kill whoever had made her cry. She was too beautiful to cry.

Since I was twenty-two I had been the alpha, and I was losing hope of finding my mate. But I finally had found her, and I didn't plan on letting her go any time soon. I'd waited long enough.

I knocked on the door and waited. I heard soft footsteps come closer and I stood up straight and cleared my throat.

She opened the door and immediately started yelling at us. "Listen. My friend and I are not in the mood, so if you could please leave that would be nice," without looking at us.

Okay. That was something I was not expecting. I was kind of expecting more of a hello or at least something along those lines.

"She's human," Zander, Jay, and Ryan said to me.

"I don't care," I said to them back in our mind-link.

"Mine," I growled softly, a little irritated by how she'd spoken to us.

"What?" she asked confused.

I pulled her to my chest. Wherever my skin was touching hers I felt sparks, and warmth spread through my entire body.

"Okay. This is a little too weird for me. So if you could let me go, that would be great," she said, trying to push me away.

I growled again.

"Mine," I pulled her back into me and breathed in her scent. My mate smelled amazing! Her hair was so soft and her eyes. Oh man, her eyes. I could get lost in them forever. I never wanted to look away. They were the perfect shade and her eye shape complemented her face perfectly.

"What is taking you so long, Sam?" girl with medium length brown hair asked as she came outside by us.

"Mine," Jay said as he pulled her into him.

"Congrats, dude," we told him as Jay snuggled closer to his mate.

He looked up and smiled. "Thanks. You too."

The girls looked at us weirdly.

"Can you please let us go?" Jay's mate asked.

"No," Jay and I said in unison.

My mate gave me a funny look then smiled.

"Fine. Shall we?" she asked turning toward her friend.

Her friend smirked evilly at us. "We shall."

What were they planning?

Little did I know, I was about to find out one way or another whether I liked it or not.

Before either of us could ask what they were talking about, they both brought their knees up and kicked us where the sun doesn't shine.

Jay and I both fell to the ground. We could hear Ryan and Zander laughing at us and the slamming of the door.

"You guys got feisty mates," Zander said.

"This ought to be quite a show," Ryan said laughing at us.

"Would you two please shut up and help us catch our mates?" I asked them while getting back up. "Shit," I cussed as I cupped myself. Damn that really hurt.

"Please?" Jay asked. Ryan and Zander groaned, but nodded.

I turned around and banged on the door.

"Leave us alone you bastards!" I heard someone yell and by Jay's growl, I'm pretty sure it was his mate.

"Seriously. Go away!" my mate yelled.

Jay joined in on the knocking and we were both about to break the door down.

"Wait," I said to Jay.

He looked confused but sniffed the air with me.

"They're outside?" he asked, confused.

We turned around and there they were watching us from behind a shed. They looked like they were having an argument of some sort.

Jay and I took off after them. Once they realized we had found them, they screamed and darted off the other way.

In about five seconds we easily caught up with them because of our wolf speed.

"Let her go!" my mate screamed when Jay picked up his mate. I grabbed my mate and stopped running. "Kyrn!" She yelled

"Sam!" Jay's mate yelled back.

"So my mate is Sam," I said to Jay smiling.

"And mine is Kyrn. Cute names," he said with the same smile.

"I agree," I said.

***

Sam

11

Oh no! We're being kidnapped, freaking kidnapped! How the hell am I going to explain this to my parents? Oh no. My parents! I'm never going to see them again. Today will be the last time I see them. Oh, you cruel world!

"Let me go, ironman," I yelled flailing around. He chuckled and shook his head. "You're laughing? I'm being kidnapped by you and you are laughing?"

"It's okay Sam. I'm not going to hurt you," he said softly.

"How do I know that? You could be a serial killer, or a psycho. Oh wait, you already are a psycho!" I shot back with a smirk.

"Trust me princess, killing you wouldn't even be an option," he said smiling down at me.

"Don't you ever call me princess again," I threatened.

"Let me go, you creeper!" I heard Kyrn yell.

I could see the brown haired boy carrying her toward the car, just as black haired guy was carrying me.

"Don't you touch her!" I yelled at the guy.

I turned in the black-haired guy's arms and kneed him in the gut. His grip loosened and I managed to wiggle my way out of his arms.

I pushed the guy over and ran to Kyrn. Once I got to her, I jumped on the guy's back, which made him release Kyrn.

"Run!" I yelled and jumped off him.

"Did you guys get them yet?" some guy asked as we pushed him and his other friend over.

"Help us grab them!" I heard someone shout behind me.

Should I be worried? I don't really care at this point because I'm too busy trying to not get kidnapped here!

"Shit!" I yelled as I was tackled, to land on the ground. I looked up at the black haired guy straddling me with my back on the ground.

He wiggled his eyebrows and smiled at the position we were in. *Oh great, he's a sick perv.*

I flailed my arms around and tried to punch him.

"Zander, grab her arms. I don't want her hurting herself." I looked up and saw this Zander guy walking toward me with an apologetic smile.

He grabbed my arms and pinned them toward the ground.

"Listen princess," he said, coming closer to my face. I glared at him and he just chuckled. "We can either do this the easy way or the hard way. But either way you are coming home with me."

I shook my head and tried to get free.

I could see the short brown haired guy straddling Kyrn's waist as well, and saw him putting a cloth to her mouth.

She slowly stopped flailing and just lay there.

"You freaking killed her! You asshole! She was my best friend!" Tears pricked my eyes.

"Sam it's okay. It was just chloroform. She'll be awake soon." The black haired guy cooed in my ear.

"Xavier, I'm taking Kyrn to the car," the Brown haired boy said.

So the psycho on top of me was Xavier. I hated to admit it, but that was a hot name. Not bad, Sam!

"Okay, Jay. I'll be there with Sam soon," Xavier said to the man who'd just put Kyrn to sleep.

"When hell freezes over!" I spat at him.

He growled and the Zander guy handed him a cloth.

Oh shit. My eyes widened in fear. "Okay I'm sorry! I'm sorry! No please don't!"

He just smirked at me. "Looks like hell *is* going to freeze over."

He placed the cloth on my mouth and I refused to breathe it in.

He noticed me not breathing and sighed.

"Come on, princess. Breathe for me. It's not going to hurt you I promise. I'm right here. Come on, Sam," he whispered gently and soothingly in my ear.

I couldn't hold my breath anymore, and breathed in the fumes.

"Good job, princess." He kissed my forehead.

My eyes closed and I felt myself being picked up, and then I was out.

I don't know how long it'd been since I fell asleep, but I started to stir and wrap the sheets around me tighter. *Damn, that was the craziest dream ever!* I laughed to myself and rolled over.

Wait. Why do the sheets smell like Axe? My eyes snapped open and I sat straight up and looked around.

I was lying in a king-sized bed in some guy's room. The walls were gray with white carpet.

Memories from last night came flooding back…seeing the four guys in the truck, being kidnapped from my house, and breathing in chloroform.

Kyrn and I had been kidnapped. *Wait, Kyrn! Where was she?*

I tried to get out of the bed, but my leg wouldn't move.

"What the hell?" I threw the covers back and saw my foot was cuffed to the bed post .I groaned in frustration and looked at it. I was in the middle of the bed, so I couldn't reach the side table.

"You have got to be kidding me! Who does this?" I asked myself as I fell back on the pillow. "Oh, that's right. Psychotic serial killers. That's who!"

Wait—my bobby pins!

I squealed in excitement as I grabbed two bobby pins out of my hair and put them both in the lock and twisted them.

I really hoped this would work. I mean it should, right? It does in Hollywood.

About three minutes later I heard a click and the handcuff came off. *Free!* I jumped off the bed and started to do my happy dance.

Now I needed to find Kyrn. I carefully walked up to the door and grabbed the handle, twisting it slowly. The door slid open and I slipped into the hallway.

I heard footsteps followed by voices.

"So, Tim, I'm guessing you have to watch over Beta Jay's mate?" a random male voice asked.

Beta? Mate? Are we in Australia or something?

"Yeah, Hunter. Are you the Luna's guard?" another male voice asked.

14

Luna? And why a guard?

"Yep. Alpha Xavier wanted me to watch over her when he isn't here. Let's go check on the Luna for him."

Alpha? What is it with all of these weird words?

Wait, they were coming my way. I turned around and ran down the hallway and jumped into a random room.

I closed the door and saw Kyrn lying on a bed, sleeping. I jumped with joy and ran over to her.

"Kyrn. Wake up.," I said shaking her.

Kyrn groaned, but opened her eyes.

"What happened? I had the weirdest dream," she said sitting up and rubbing her eyes. "I dreamed you and I were kidnapped by these four really sexy guys and...," her voice trailed off as she looked around the room.

"Yeah. That wasn't a dream," I said, laughing at her.

"Oh," she whispered. "Uh. Why is my foot cuffed to the bed?" She pointed to it.

"I don't know; mine was too. But thanks to my bobby pins, I'm free," I said with a huge smile.

"Could you please get it off?" she asked hopefully.

I smacked the back of her head. "Of course I will. I'm not going to leave you here!" I did the same thing with her lock and it clicked open.

"Thanks," she said, rubbing her ankle. "How are we going to get out of here?"

"I don't know," I walked to the window and looked across the landscape.

"We drive," I said pointing to the open garage.

"That could work. But how do we get out of this house. Because I am so not walking out of this room...they'll catch us for sure," Kyrn said, depressed.

"I don't know," I said back to her.

"Wait," she walked toward the window. "We can climb out this," she said opening it up.

"We are on the second story." I sounded as scared as I felt.

"Then we drop. I'm not staying in our kidnappers' house. Even if they are hot. It's not going to happen, Sam."

"Oh, their names are Xavier, Jay, Ryan, and Zander. My guy is Xavier, yours is Jay, the shaggy blond haired guy is Zander, and the other guy is Ryan. I heard them say each other's names last night. And there are the other guys, Hunter and Tim," I explained. "I heard them when I sneaked out of my room"

"Okay, at least we have names. Now let's go," she said as she shoved me toward the window.

I nodded in defeat, and set my feet out the window.

"We got this Kyrn," I said, holding her hand

"What the hell?"

We turned around to see Xavier and Jay looking pissed. And Ryan and Zander with amused smiles.

"Jump?" Kyrn asked me.

"Yup," I said. "Kiss our asses!" I yelled before we jumped out.

"Sam! Get back here!" I heard Xavier yell.

"Kyrn!" Jay yelled.

I whimpered in pain as I landed on the ground. I rolled on my side and stood up.

"Shit that hurt," Kyrn groaned as we hobbled our way to the garage. "Come on, Sam."

Don't have to tell me twice.

"What car?" I asked frantically as I tried to keep pressure off my ankle.

"Just pick one!" Kyrn yelled at me.

We ran to an orange Lamborghini and I hopped in the driver's seat.

"Sweet! The keys are in the ignition. These people are stupid." I laughed as I keyed it on.*Seriously—what are the odds that this would actually happen? Not very good I tell you, for sure.*I put the car in reverse and pulled out of the garage, almost hitting Xavier and Jay on the way out. I laughed at them, but they looked really pissed off.

"Suck on that!" Kyrn and I yelled at the same time.

I was driving through the forest when I saw a red object behind us.

"Shit, they are following us. And they are gaining on us quick," Kyrn worried.

"Oh my gosh!" I cried out.

"What?" she asked me.

"I can cross off being in a car chase from my bucket list!" I said smiling.

"Oh my gosh, Sam." She shook her head.

"What? It's something I've always wanted to do," I smiled.

Kyrn nodded. "I know that. I just can't believe you can actually cross it off."

I laughed and swerved so I didn't hit a tree. "By any chance, do you happen to know where we are?"

Kyrn sighed. "Sadly no. But we have to get out of the forest."

I nodded. "Well, the good news is that we are on a trail. Which means there has to be a road close by."

"Let's just hurry up and find it before they catch up to us."

'I couldn't agree more with you, Kyrn.' I took a sharp left and drifted a little until I got full control of the car. This was not how I was going to die.

Chapter 3: So Close

Sam

"Where did they go?" I asked Kyrn.

"I don't know. I haven't seen them for ten minutes," she said looking around.

"Okay," whispered to myself as I finally hopped onto a road. Where it led, I had no idea. But I would rather drive on this road than stay in the forest with those kidnappers.

I kept driving and about an hour later we arrived at some small town.

"I'm hungry," Kyrn whined for the tenth time. I told her we needed to keep driving and once we got to a safe distance, we would stop and get something to eat. But she didn't shut up about it.

"Okay." I laughed giving in. "We can pull over at a McDonalds or something."

"Sounds good to me," Kyrn mumbled as her stomach growled.

I smiled in victory as I saw a giant golden 'M'.

"Look, there's one." I pulled into the parking lot.

"Let's get food, then find a train ticket or something," Kyrn said as I nodded in agreement.

"Hello ladies. Can I help you?" A red-haired boy asked us with a flirty smile as soon we walked in and closed the door.

"Watch this," she whispered to me. "Hey. We lost our purses and we don't have any money. But we were wondering if you would be kind enough to give us water?" she asked softly looking shy.

I chuckled with a smirk as he kept his eyes fixed on Kyrn. I loved it when she did this. 'Hello free food!'

"You girls order anything you like. It's on me. My name's Luke," he said extending his hand toward us.

"My name is Kyrn. And this is my best friend Sam."

"Hi," I smiled sweetly, shaking his hand.

"So, what would you girls like?" Luke asked us as he tried to look cool. Sorry bud. It's not really working for you.

"My usual," I told Kyrn.

"Two McChickens, medium fries, and two large sprites?" Kyrn told Luke as he tapped away on the screen.

"Okay. For here or to go?" Luke asked us.

Kyrn was about to reply but I tapped her shoulder and she looked at me.

I pointed at the window and there they were. The four boys. How the hell did they find us?

"To go, please," Kyrn said in a rush.

"Are you girls okay?" Luke asked us, concerned.

"Yeah, we're just in a hurry. So, we'll take it to go. Please," I told him.

"Oh. Of course," he said as he scrambled to get our orders.

A couple minutes passed and the guys hadn't moved.

Thankfully I'd parked the Lamborghini on the other side, so they couldn't see us.

"Here you are," Luke said handing us our bags and drinks.

"Thank you for everything." Kyrn and I kissed his cheeks.

His face turned a bright shade of red.

"Umm you're welcome," he said nervously with a small smile.

I giggled and Kyrn opened the door.

"And that is how you do it," Kyrn smirked as we ran to the car.

"Come on." I laughed. "Let's go now so they can't see us."

We hopped in the car and the boys still weren't paying attention. "Next stop, train station," Kyrn said.

The drive to the nearest train station was a lot longer than I thought. I guess that's what happens when you're in a small town.

They don't have a lot of anything. We barely saw a grocery store, and maybe one or two gas stations. That's it. And they weren't even that big really.

By the time we did find a train station, it was already getting dark.

"Let's just leave the keys in the car. We won't be back for them any time soon," Kyrn laughed as we parked the car.

I nodded and quickly got out of the car. The faster we moved, the faster we'd get away from here.

"Why is it so empty?" I asked as I opened the door.

"It's another small town Sam. It's going to be empty," Kyrn responded. I nodded as we ran up to the counter.

"Can your flirt your way through again?" I asked her.

"Yeah. It shouldn't be a problem. But if I need help, I'm calling for you," she smiled.

"Hello ladies," the guys said, smiling at us. "How can I help you?"

"Please. I think my friend and I are being followed. We need two train tickets far, far away from here immediately," Kyrn said acting scared. She was pretty good. This was why I was so proud to call her my best friend.

The guy looked at me and I pretended to cry.

"But Kyrn. We lost our purses remember?" I said to her.

"Shit. I guess we'll have to walk," she said looking down. "Come on, Sam."

She grabbed my hand and turned around.

"Wait!" the guy called out.

Kyrn gave me a mischievous smile, but dropped it once she turned around to face the man.

"Here. They're on the house," the guy said with two tickets in his hand.

"Thank you," Kyrn said kissing his cheek.

I could have sworn I heard a growl.

"Thank you so much sir," I said kissing his other cheek.

There it is again. Am I going crazy? I looked around, but didn't see anything. I must be.

"Are you okay?" Kyrn asked in concern.

Here we are running for our lives from psychotic kidnappers, but other than that I'm perfectly fine.

"Let's head out," I said letting it slide.

Kyrn nodded and followed me out the door. We only took one step before we were grabbed from behind. I tried to scream but a hand went over my mouth.

Shit. Being kidnapped again. Can I ever catch a break?

"Fancy seeing you here, princess," Xavier said brushing his lips on my ear.

I shivered and held in a gasp. I looked over at Kyrn and saw that Jay had her. She looked scared and frankly, I was too. We both noticed each other's fears and glared at the guys opposite us.

Xavier laughed. "Come on princess. Let's get you home," he said picking me up bridal style.

Home? Did he really just say home? Does he honestly think that where he took us is our 'home'? News flash Xavier. My home is my own house. Not the place you're taking us to.

"Meet you at the house, Xavier," Jay said picking Kyrn up. "I'm going to go get my Lamborghini Sam and Kyrn stole."

"Then maybe you shouldn't have kidnapped us, idiot," Kyrn said slapping his face, knocking that stupid glare off his stupid face.

I held in a laugh that needed to so desperately come out. Xavier tried to cover up a laugh, but I slapped him as well and got out of his arms.

"That goes for you too, idiot," I said glaring at him.

He glared at me and trapped my arms behind my back. "Let's go," he said pulling me toward the Ferrari.

"No. Let go of me!" I shouted trying to get anyone's attention.

"Stop struggling, Sam," he commanded in a low voice.

I froze and he picked me up again. There was so much power behind his voice, it scared me. He pushed me into his car and shut the door. I immediately went over to it and tried to open the door, but failed. I heard his door open and he laughed.

"Child lock. Gotta love it huh?" He smirked.

I glared at him and pulled my hoodie over my head and curled up into a ball. I closed my eyes and let the tears fall. 'I can't believe this is really happening to me. What's going to happen to me?'

***

I must have dozed off or something because I felt myself being picked up. I opened one eye and Xavier was carrying me back in the house. He looked down and I quickly closed my eye. I felt his laugh vibrate through his chest.

After a couple of minutes of walking, he set me down on a bed. I slowly opened my eyes to see him taking his pants and shirt off.

"W-what are you d-doing?" I asked wide-eyed. *Oh no. H-he's not going to rape me, is he?*

My eyes raked over his arms, his chest, and then his eight-pack. *Stupid mind!* He smirked and climbed in the bed next to where I was sitting.

"Going to bed," he simply stated. I huffed and tried to stand up.

He put an arm around my waist, pulling me beside him, and sighed as I tried to break free from his grasp.

"I'm sorry Sam," he said sadly as he kissed the back of my neck.

"Why?" I asked him.

"Why what?" he asked confused.

"Why did you kidnap me?" My voiced cracked at the end as I turned to look at his face.

"I can't tell you," he said quietly.

"Why?"

"I will tell you when the time is right."

"But why not now?"

"Because."

"Because why?"

"I just can't."

"And why—

"Please Sam. You need some sleep, and I do too," he sounded desperate.

"Fine," I said through clenched teeth as I turned to face the wall again. He pulled me more into him and I elbowed his gut.

"Don't touch me," I warned as I scooted farther away from him, but that only caused him to pull me back to his warm strong chest.

"Don't scoot away from me," he said in a low voice.

"I can if I want to," I spat at him. "You don't own me!"

"Sam, I mean it. And don't think that you escaping will go unpunished. You are in a lot of trouble for doing that. And don't ever, and I mean *ever* run away from me again," he said turning me to face him.

"Whatever," I scoffed.

"And I'm only going to say this Samantha…"

My name sounded so good rolling off of his tongue—no, bad Sam. Keep it together.

"I like you Sam, so that means you are mine. No boy can touch you the way I can, look at you the way I can, and kiss you only the way I can," he growled.

What is up with this dude growling? Like seriously, I think he needs to go get his throat checked out.

"You can't do that," I said staring at him in utter shock.

"Oh yes I can." And with that he crashed his lips on mine.

He kissed me! This freaking stranger-kidnapper-psycho-creeper-stalker kissed me!

But it did feel so nice to have his lips moving against mine. It felt like a million fireworks going off and butterflies were swarming around in my stomach.

What am I thinking? I'm not supposed to be enjoying this what so ever.

I moved my lips against his and I felt him smile and he pulled me closer. He pulled back after a minute and kissed my forehead.

"Goodnight, my princess."

After realizing what just happened, I turned around and pulled the covers closer to me. He laughed and kept his arm securely wrapped around my waist.

This didn't change anything; I was still going to get the hell out of here. I didn't care what it took. Kyrn and I were leaving and that was that.

Chapter 4: What's The Plan, Sam

Sam

I woke up and stretched. Thank you, sun. *Note the sarcasm in that statement.* I realized I couldn't move, and looked down to see an arm draped across my stomach, and my back was pressed against a warm firm chest I squeezed my eyes shut and hoped to God that this was a dream and it wasn't real.

But when I reopened my eyes and that large strong arm was still there, I sighed in defeat. *Of course it's not a dream. Why would it be. knowing my luck?* I tried wiggling free, but the arm tightened and kept me in place. I couldn't move at all and this was starting to get really annoying. I groaned heavily and tried to shove the arm off me one last time.

"You're awake," I heard a deep sexy voice come from behind me.

"And you're a psycho," I snipped at him.

He turned me around so I was facing him. "Watch how you talk to me."

"Whatever you say, *your highness,*" I said in a very sassy tone. I could tell he was getting annoyed and I smirked at the thought I was getting under his skin. *You want to make my life hell; I'll make your life hell.*

"Don't test me, princess," Xavier warned in a low tone.

On second thought, I probably shouldn't provoke my kidnapper, I mean he could kill me right now if he wanted to. So I did the best thing and kept my mouth shut. But not without throwing a glare his way. "Now I have to go do some pa-I mean work," he said nervously.

Hiding something, are we Mr. Kidnapper?

"So can you stay here and behave like a good girl?" he asked as he sat up and rubbed his eyes.

I faked a smile. I so wanted to stab him. But if I was going to escape, I need him gone, and now.

"Yes sir," I teased with a fake salute.

He narrowed his eyes and got up from the bed and headed to the bathroom.

As I was running through my plan in my head, he came out of the bathroom ten minutes later, just in jeans with his hair dripping wet. And might I say, he looked damn good. My eyes traveled to his arms, then his chest, then his abs. *Oh my gosh those abs!* My hormones were all over the place. My eyes continued down to his V line and then the rest was covered by his dark blue jeans.

"Are you done eye-raping me yet?" Xavier asked with such a smirk plastered on his sexy ass face that I desperately wanted to punch it off.

I snapped out of my thoughts and looked him in the eyes which were a darker mossy green and held amusement in them.

I scoffed at him. "I was not."

"Princess, let's face it. You totally were." He chuckled.

"Whatever gets you to sleep at night," I said brushing past him and going into the bathroom and locking the door.

"Fine. I got to go. And don't bother trying to get out of the house. I have Hunter and Tim downstairs," he shouted so I could hear him.

I groaned but stayed quiet. I heard the bedroom door open and close again so I decided to jump in the shower. I was done in about twenty minutes. I hopped out, putting on my clothes again. I know it was gross, but I didn't really have anything else to wear, and I wasn't wearing Xavier's clothes.

When I got out, I went to the room Kyrn was in last time and found her flicking through the channels.

"Hey," she said, looking at me and scooting over on the bed to make room for me.

"Hey." I lay down next to her and stared at the ceiling.

"How are we going to get out of here? Jay said something about don't bother because Tim and Hunter are downstairs," Kyrn said confused.

I sat up and rested on my elbows. "Yeah. Xavier told me the same thing."

"So, what's the plan, Sam?"

"Well when I was in the shower, I was thinking—"

"Eew, gross! I don't need to know those things," she said looking completely grossed out.

"Kyrn!" I yelled hitting her in the head. "Oh my gosh no! I was thinking of a plan, you blithering idiot!"

"O-ohh. That makes more sense now," she laughed while holding the back of her head.

"Ya think? Anyway, if we can find a door with a lock on the outside, then we can somehow lure them in there and shut the door. And boom! They are locked in the house and we are free."

"Sounds good to me. But how do we do this?" Kyrn asked as she shut the TV off.

"We need to find the right kind of door first," I laughed slightly. "We go in there and hide, then when we hear them coming, we come out of our hiding spot, rush out and lock them in there."

"Okay. Let's go," she said getting up from the bed.

We quietly made our way out of the room and slowly crept downstairs.

"Oh come on, Bears! You are facing the Cowboys. Kick their ass!" I heard someone yell.

"Calm down, Tim. Geez."

So that was Tim and the one talking must be Hunter then.

"Sorry. But they need to win," we heard Tim say.

"Bears suck," I whispered to Kyrn.

"Let's go find a room." Kyrn laughed as she pulled me by my shirt. We made our way through the house trying to find the door with the lock.

"Hey," Kyrn called to me.

I turned around and she was pointing to a door with a lock on the outside.

"It's a basement. We can hide down there and wait until they come when we scream," Kyrn suggested.

"Okay," I said as I opened the door.

"Wow," Kyrn and I gawked when we made it to the last step looking at all of the weapons.

"Is it bad that I'm completely terrified right now?" she asked me.

"Nope," I said popping the 'p'. "Because I am too."

"Okay. I'm glad I'm not the only one," Kyrn gulped.

We looked around for a few more minutes before she spoke up.

"Hey, didn't you take a self-defense class on how to use sais?"

"Yeah. Why?" I asked walking over to her.

"Well, here you go," she said smiling. "And they come with holsters you can strap on your chest."

I picked up a pair and smiled widely. I took my sweatshirt off and put the holsters on and put the sais in them. I tested them out, and it was perfect. *I can't wait to use these. Tim and Hunter, you two are going down.*

I put my sweatshirt back on and looked for a weapon for Kyrn.

"Here, I know how much you like knives," I said giving a pair of daggers.

"O-oh, and they come with holsters too, to wrap around your ankles," she said giggling and put them on.

"Now we have our weapons, shall we scream?" I ask her in a posh tone.

"Let's," she said in the same accent. "Turn the lights off and hide under the stairs. Then when they come running down, we can sneak out and lock the door."

"Okay. And I'm starting to think these guys aren't regular kidnappers. I mean seriously, they have a basement full of weapons!"

"I know!" she said as we made our way under the stairs.

"Three, two, one," I counted down and we screamed. When we stopped screaming, we heard footsteps scrambling around upstairs.

"What was that?" a frantic male voice asked.

"Doesn't that sound like Ryan?" I asked Kyrn in a whisper.

"Did someone scream?" another male voice asked.

"I don't know, you idiot. We have to check it out. It could be the girls. I think it came from downstairs," some mumbled.

"And there is Hunter and Tim," Kyrn said with a mischievous smile.

Footsteps were coming closer, and I matched her smile. They stopped right in front of the door.

"They are in the basement; their scent says they are definitely down here," Tim said, scared.

"Our scent?" Kyrn whispered to me.

I shrugged and continued to listen.

"What are they doing down here with all of the weapons?" Ryan asked worried.

"How am I supposed to know? We'll go check it out and make sure they aren't hurt. Alpha Xavier and Beta Jay would not be happy with us," Hunter said.

"Alpha and Beta?" Kyrn asked me.

"I heard the same thing earlier the other day," I told her. "Hunter and Tim kept talking about it, but I couldn't get anything useful from their conversation."

They were walking downstairs and thankfully kept walking.

I nudged Kyrn and we sneaked out and quietly walked up the stairs.

"Where are they?" I heard Hunter ask.

"I don't know. Let's go back upstairs," Tim said. "They might not have been in the basement."

We quickly shut the door and locked it.

"Grab the chair!" I yelled to Kyrn.

She grabbed it and I put it under the doorknob so they couldn't turn it.

"Hey! Let us out!" Ryan yelled.

"No can do! Sorry," I laughed.

29

"Sam!" Hunter yelled.

"Yes?" I asked innocently.

"You need to open this door."

"Sorry dude. She can't do that," Kyrn joined in.

"Kyrn!" Tim yelled.

"Sorry. Please leave a message after the beep." She paused for affect. "BEEEEEEEP!"

Kyrn and I nearly fell to the floor laughing.

"Let's go before the other psycho kidnappers show up," I said getting up slowly.

Kyrn nodded while she got up herself and we walked to the front door.

We opened the door and took two steps before we were stopped by these huge guys. And I do mean huge.

"Hello. And where are you going?" the guy on the left asked with an Irish accent.

"Shit. They are with them," Kyrn whispered to me when the guy was focused on me.

I nodded, understanding what she was saying.

Come on, think Sam, we need to get out of here. Oh wait. I have an idea!

"A walk," I said smiling.

"Sorry. You can't do that," the guy in the right said with a southern accent.

I looked at Kyrn but she was one step ahead of me.

"Xavier and Jay said we could," Kyrn said lying smoothly.

"They did?" he asked obviously confused.

"Yeah. Why would I lie to some guy I just met? I don't have a reason to lie; you guys didn't do anything bad to me," she said in a d'uh tone.

"Oh. Okay then, just not too far from the house and be back here in ten minutes," he warned with a stern look.

"Okay. Thanks," I said smiling at him before I walked away.

I waited till we were out of ear range so they wouldn't hear us.

"Nice." I laughed giving her a high five.

"Why thank you. Thank you very much," she said in a fake posh tone and added a little bow at the end.

We continued walking until we found a pathway a couple of minutes later.

"You know our ten minutes is up right?" I turned to face Kyrn.

"Yeah, I know." She sighed.

"I wonder if they'll send someone after us." I stopped to look around, then started walking again once I hadn't seen anyone coming after us.

"Me-"

"Sam and Kyrn!"

We stopped walking and shut our eyes. Oh, please be the police or something.

When we unfroze ourselves, we turned around and saw Ryan, Hunter, and Tim standing there, arms crossed over their chests, and angry expressions dancing on their faces.

How did the hell did they get out?

"Oh," I started.

"Shit," Kyrn finished for me.

We looked at each other scared.

She gulped. "Ready to fight?"

I nodded and took off my sweatshirt to reveal the sais.

She pulled up her pants legs and folded them over so the holsters were showing.

Ryan smirked. "Looks like they really were in the basement."

"Do they know how to use them?" Hunter asked nervously.

"I highly doubt it. They're just girls after all," Tim said smiling.

Rude much?

"Shall we put them to shame?" I asked Kyrn.

She nodded.

"Actually. We *do* know how to use them. I took a martial arts class that specialized in using weapons. I happened to pick the one that used sais, and stuck with it for two and a half years," I said with a smirk as the guys gulped.

"And I took the one with daggers, for the same amount of time," Kyrn said proudly.

"We are in deep shit," Ryan mumbled.

I could have sworn I heard Tim say something about why can't he use his other form. But I could be wrong.

"Come and get us," Kyrn and I said drawing our weapons.

Chapter 5: Kicking Ass and Flashbacks

Sam

The guys looked hesitant, and stared at each other.

"They're having a mental conversation or something," Kyrn said in a whisper.

"They do look like they are.. And their eyes look different," I pointed out as we looked closer.

Their eyes were foggy. It was quite strange actually.

"Well, they look like they are spacing out. So, want to run?" she asked, laughing and putting her daggers back in the holster.

"Hell, yeah," I smiled, and did the same thing with my Sais.

We tiptoed backwards before setting off in a dead sprint.

"Hey!" We heard behind us.

"Ah!" I heard Kyrn scream. I stopped running and turned around to see her being tackled to the ground by Tim.

"Get off of her, you freak!" I said charging him and wrapping my arms around his waist while still moving forward.

"Damn, this girl has a strong grip," Tim said struggling under me.

"Don't even think about it!" Kyrn yelled.

I turned around just in time to see her trip Hunter, who was running toward me.

"You're welcome," she said smiling at me.

I smiled back and turned to Tim.

I quickly grabbed the rope we'd got from the basement and tied his wrists together.

He looked at me wide eyed.

I smiled innocently at him.

"You lose," I said getting off him, and saw Hunter tied up too.

"Nicely done," I said giving Kyrn a high five.

"So, what did you say about us being just girls?" Kyrn asked a scared looking Ryan.

"But... I... you... girls!" He growled at us but not very loud.

"What is up with you guys growling? I mean honestly. You guys really need to get your throats checked," I said looking concerned at him.

He laughed. "My throat's fine, Sam."

"You sure? I mean all of you guys are growling and it's weird," I mumbled as he laughed again and got in a fighting stance.

"Enough with the chit chat. You girls are coming back to the house," he said with a smile.

"Ha! That's what you think," Kyrn said smirking at him.

"Ready to kick our kidnapper's ass?" I asked her.

"Oh yeah," she replied back getting her daggers out.

"Then let's do this," I said grabbing my Sais.

Kyrn charged while I slipped behind him when he was too focused on blocking Kyrn's knives.

I got a running start and drop kicked him in his back. Kyrn helped me as back-up and we ran at him.

He got up with inhuman speed which shocked us both. He looked nervous but quickly masked it before he swiped my feet from underneath me. He went to grab my wrist but I rolled to the left at the last minute.

While he was facing the ground, Kyrn jumped on his back and put a knife through his shirt, so he was trapped to the ground. Then she did the same with the other side and pushed his face to the ground.

"Okay. Before we leave, we want to know why you guys kidnapped us," I demanded as I kneeled beside his head that was still smashed in the ground.

Kyrn grabbed his head so his cheek was pressed up against the ground.

He coughed and sighed. "I can't tell you."

"Why is everyone saying that?" I groaned.

"It's not my place to tell."

"Then who's is it?" Kyrn asked pushing his cheek to the ground harder.

"I can't tell you that either. You girls aren't ready for it," Ryan mumbled.

What are they hiding?

"We just kicked your guys' asses! I'm pretty sure we are ready," I yelled at him.

He flinched from my sudden outburst.

His eyes looked foggy again and I nudged Kyrn.

"Look," I said pointing to his eyes. "We need to get out of here. I don't like this place."

She nodded and quickly, silently grabbed her knives.

We put our weapons back in the holsters and turned around to run. But not before running into a wall.

Why is a wall out here in the middle of nowhere?

I slowly looked up and saw Xavier with his arms crossed.

"Shit," I mumbled under my breath.

"Shit is right," he said in a stern voice.

How did he hear that? I think these guys are hiding something big.

"So, how did the girls manage to get you on the ground and Tim and Hunter tied up?" Jay asked, angry.

"Believe it or not, give the girls a weapon and they will kick major ass," Ryan said dusting himself off.

Xavier and Jay turned to Tim and Hunter, and they nodded their heads.

Xavier pinched the bridge of his nose and sighed.

"I told you to make sure they didn't escape. And here we are, miles from the house and they almost escaped. Again!" His voice boomed.

"Sorry al-" Ryan, Tim, and Hunter started, but was interrupted.

"Yes, Xavier," Jay cut off their sentence.

Kyrn and I shared a confused look, but didn't say anything. What were they going to say?

"Let's go," Xavier said grabbing my upper arm.

Before his grip got any tighter, I yanked my arm back. I pulled out my Sais, out and took a defensive stance.

Xavier looked at me, his eyes now black. And when I mean black, I mean pitch black.

"I'm not going anywhere with you, you psycho," I said through clenched teeth.

Xavier gave me a hard glare before speaking. "Yes. You. Will."

"No. I. Won't," I said as he took a step toward me and I backed up raising my Sais. "Don't come near me."

Kyrn took this as an advantage; she jumped around him, coming to my side and drew her knives.

"Kyrn. Get over here now," Jay commanded.

"No," she said raising her knives.

Jay's eyes went pitch black, and he moved right next to Xavier.

"Put down your weapons," Xavier said in a powerful tone.

The guys, even Jay, whimpered a little at his tone; I froze, along with Kyrn.

He smirked and took a step toward me.

I got out of my Trans at the last minute and swiftly moved my right Sais toward his reached out hand.

He hissed in pain and brought his hand back.

"I said, don't come near me," I yelled as he studied me for a minute before smiling.

"Fine. You want to fight, then let's go. Jay," he said turning to him.

Jay nodded and they both took their shirts off.

"Oh, this isn't fair. It's going to be hard to not concentrate on that," I whispered to Kyrn so they wouldn't hear us.

But by the smug looks they had on their faces, I'm pretty sure they heard.

"Come on princess. You make the first move," he said and he flexed his arms. *There he goes, using that stupid little nickname again.*

But those muscles... Snap out of it Sam. He's only doing this to get you to lose focus.

Oh my gosh, I just want to lick—

"Princess? You there?"

"Huh, what?" I asked.

"Are you going to make the first move?" he asked, a little slower, as if I were stupid.

"I'm not stupid, you idiot," I spat at him. "I heard you the first time."

His face went from amusement to anger.

"Jay, focus on your girl, and I'll focus on mine," Jay nodded and locked eyes with Kyrn.

"Excuse me. But we are not your girls," I said as Kyrn nodded in agreement.

"Actually princess, you are. You're mine, just as Kyrn is Jay's," Xavier said.

"I'm not Jay's," Kyrn said bitterly.

A flash of hurt went through Jay's eyes, but he masked it the second it came.

"And I'm not yours," I said to Xavier.

Hurt went through his eyes as well, but it stayed there a little bit longer before he covered it up.

"That's where you're wrong, princess," Xavier said before running toward me. He went to grab me around my waist, but I twirled and dodged his flying arms.

I turned all the way around and kicked at his leg. He didn't stay down long; he got right back up, and I narrowed my eyes at him. I then realized he was going to be a whole lot harder to fight than the other guys.

He charged me again, and successfully knocked me to the ground when I wasn't paying attention to him. I hissed in pain when my back made contact with the dirt.

Xavier looked worried, but it went away when I hopped back up and swung at him, barely missing his head.

"You're pretty good, princess," he said smiling at me.

"You're not too bad yourself," I said back with a small smile.

He was in front of me in seconds—and he'd been just less than twenty feet from me.

"How did you—" But before I could finish, he had me pinned to the ground with my arms above my head, straddling me.

"You know now what I think about it. I'm really enjoying being in this position with you princess," he said wiggling his eyebrows.

"You sick perv!" I screamed in his face.

His face dropped, and I instantly felt guilty.

Wait, why am I feeling guilty?

"I'm only twenty-two!" he shouted back.

I shrank back at his voice and he noticed. His eyes softened and I immediately felt a little bit better. But for some reason it hurt that he yelled at me. I shrugged it off for now.

"And I'm eighteen," I mumbled.

Wait. Why did I tell him my age? What the hell is wrong with me?

"That's not bad. At least you're legal," he said with a suggestive wink.

"Oh my gosh. You are a perv!"

He huffed as he looked away from me. "Whatever."

I used this as an advantage and kicked him off me.

"Ah!" he yelped as he hit the ground.

I put my knees in the crook of his elbows, and put one sai above his head so he couldn't move, and the other at his throat.

"Nice job Sam," I heard Jay say. He had Kyrn pinned to the ground.

My mouth gaped open and the next thing I knew I was pinned to the ground with my arms by my head, my Sais about five feet away from me.

"You asshole!" I yelled.

"Sorry Sam," Xavier smiled. "I needed you to think you had the upper hand and waited for the perfect time for you to get distracted."

He leaned his head down, closer by the second.

I froze because I didn't know what to do. So I decided to fake a sneeze and he jumped slightly and pulled back.

He knew it wasn't real and sighed.

"Bless you," he mumbled.

"Uh, thanks," I said turning my head and letting out a nervous laugh. Oh, this isn't totally awkward.

He got off me but not before handcuffing our wrists together. I gasped at the handcuff and went to go yell at him but he quickly covered my mouth with his hand.

"No more cussing. We can't have those bad words coming out of that little pretty mouth of yours," he said as I blushed furiously and the ground suddenly became very interesting. *Another handcuff? What is this guy? A cop?*

"Ready to go home Xavier?" Jay asked.

I looked over and met Kyrn's sad eyes. My eyes traveled down her arm and saw that she was in the same predicament I was in. I met her sad eyes again and saw a tear slip out.

Anger bubbled up inside me and I picked up a rock and chucked it at Jay's head. It hit him straight in the forehead, and he groaned holding his head.

Kyrn gasped and looked at me in shock.

Jay growled at me and met my eyes. "What the hell was that for?"

"For making her cry, you asshole!" I spat at him, my anger growing. If you can't tell, I'm extremely overprotective of her.

We might both be eighteen, but I'm older than her by a couple of months. I was born in May and she was born in November. We've been best friends since we were both two years old. We have always been there for each other, and we have told each other everything. I was there for her first breakup and she was there for mine. I was there when Trey cheated on her, and she was here when Brett cheated on me. We always have each other's backs, even if we don't need them. We are always there for each other.

I leapt at him, but Xavier held me back. His eyes softened and he immediately turned toward Kyrn.

He looked pained as he brought a hand up to her face and wiped the tear away.

She flinched and I knew why.

Trey hit her, before, and she'd always been terrified to date after that, because she didn't want to relive it. I remember when she came over to my house right after that, and I told her to stay there and I went over to Trey's house.

When I knocked on his door and I saw his face, I saw red. I immediately launched myself toward him and knocked him to the ground. I repeatedly punched him in the face, and that also was the first time he punched me. I didn't know if it was for self-defense, or if he meant it just like he did when he slapped Kyrn.

I remember going home that night and having Kyrn clean up my busted lip from where Trey punched me. I wanted to call the cops but Kyrn begged me not to because she still loved him. And Trey knew that, so he used it to his advantage. I finally talked some sense into her and she broke up with him. Ever since then, she's been afraid to date. And odd enough, Brett and Trey were cousins.

Brett never hit me, but he would become extremely jealous over the smallest things and he has raised his voice at me a lot. It happened one day on our date and when he went up to use the restroom, the waiter asked me if he wanted to know if I was okay and if anything has happened. I knew what he was referring to, but I politely shook my head. He nodded and left before Brett came back.

When Jay saw her flinch he looked confused, but I could feel my face going red in anger.

"Don't you dare touch her," I said through gritted teeth.

Kyrn noticed how I was acting and gave me a small smile in gratitude.

"Sam, what's wrong?" Xavier asked me.

"Nothing," I said calmly trying to burn a hole in Jay's head. Sadly it wasn't working.

"Sam, it's okay," Kyrn said in her soft voice. I nodded an okay, but still glared at him.

"I'm sorry. It's just you know how I am. Ever since that day…" I clamped my free hand over my mouth and stopped myself from talking.

"That day?" Jay asked confused. "What happened?"

Kyrn and I looked at each other.

"N-nothing," she stuttered.

"What. Happened?" Jay asked

"Nothing happened," she said calmly.

"But Sam just said—"

"So. Aren't you guys supposed to be taking us prisoners back to the dungeon?" I asked trying to lighten the mood.

The guys sighed and nodded walking in the direction of the house.

I smiled at Kyrn and she smiled warmly back at me as we made our way back 'home.'

The walk was very quiet. A couple of conversations here and there between Jay and Xavier and the guys, but that was about it. They tried to get us to talk, but we were giving them the silent treatment. There was no way in hell I was going to talk to either of them. I wanted to kill them both . Well, mostly Jay. But I had to wait because of these stupid handcuffs.

When we got back to the house, Xavier led me up the stairs to the same room I'd woken up in. He handcuffed me to the bed right as we stepped into his room.

I still had bobby pins in my hair and I planned on using those when he left.

"What the hell were you thinking?" he asked, pacing around his room.

"Hmm, I don't know. Maybe getting away from the psycho guys who kidnapped us!" I spoke in my d'uh tone. *It should be obvious why we ran. To me it was. I don't really know about this idiot standing in front of me.*

"You are unbelievable."

"At least I didn't kidnap someone from their home!"

He groaned. "It had to be done. I was planning on doing it at the stop light but you zoomed off."

"Well I'm glad the light changed then," I said with a smirk.

"Speaking of which, why were you crying?" His voice was dead serious now.

I looked down and felt tears making their way through and they wanted to be shown. A tear slipped through and before I could wipe it away, Xavier put his finger under my chin and lifted my head up. He put his hand on my cheek and wiped the tear away with his thumb.

"Are you okay, baby?" he asked, concerned.

Baby? Where did 'baby' come from?

"I'm fine," my voice was shaking.

Flashbacks started going through my mind and I couldn't stop them.

***

I made my way to his house and parked my car in his driveway. I opened the door and went upstairs to give him our two-year anniversary present.

I opened the door and walked in.

"Hey Brett, I got-oh my gosh," the last part came out in a whisper. When I walked in, I noticed a very naked Brett, on top of a very naked Tasha, and they were...uh...getting it on.

"I love you, Tasha," he says leaning down and kissing her.

I cleared my throat and he quickly looked up; when his eyes landed on me with my arms crossed, they widened. "Oh my gosh. Sam baby, when did you get here?" he asked quickly and got off Tasha.

"Hey Sam, I was just uh—" Tasha started but I cut her off.

"Shut up." She quickly looked down and wrapped the sheets around herself tighter.

I looked at the picture and grabbed the tickets out of the picture frame before I threw it on the ground.

The glass shattered and Tasha gasped.

"Happy two-year anniversary 'boyfriend'," He looked at me with so much regret and a tear slipped out. I held both football tickets in front of him and ripped them, in his face. His eyes widened. "Go to hell," I said before I ran out of there.

I ran downstairs and out the door to my car and hopped in.

Brett came running out of his house and knocked on my window.

"Please baby, let me explain," he begged.

"There is nothing to explain. We are over! I hate you," I whispered the last part and rushed out his driveway and headed home.

* * *

"Are you okay?" Xavier asked me.

"Yeah. I'm fine," I lied.

"Sam. Please don't lie to me. I can tell when you are lying to me."

I looked down, not wanting him to see the tears. "I'm not ready to talk just yet." The only person who knew was Kyrn. And she will always be the only one to know and the first to know about everything.

He nodded and leaned in again.

I panicked and quickly turned around on the bed so I was facing away from him. I heard him sigh in frustration and he sounded a little hurt.

I don't get why he was so hurt though. Who kisses a random stranger they've kidnapped?

He unlocked the handcuff, thankfully, and climbed into his bed next to me, pulling me to him.

That's when I realized he didn't have on a shirt—I could feel his bare back against my arms.

I felt my eyes close. and soon enough I was sound asleep.

Xavier

I couldn't help but wonder what had happened in her past, and why was she crying. And I'd also seen the protective nature she was giving off when Jay touched Kyrn's cheek.

I felt proud to have her as my mate. She would make the perfect Luna.

I do need her to love me first. but she keeps running away.

"Well maybe if you stop keeping her locked up all the time and treat her like a person instead of a prisoner, she will warm up to us." My wolf scowled me.

"Oh shut up. I'm doing this for a reason. And you were all for it when I kidnapped her," I shot back

"That's because I need to have my mate by us."

"So? You were still for it."

"Whatever. Just get her to warm up to us. I want to mark her and claim her already," he whined.

"And I don't? That's all I can think about."

"Well hurry up."

"I'm trying." I shut him off and listen to my mate's shallow breathing which meant she was asleep.

I nuzzled my face in her neck and breathed in deeply. I smiled, and soon fell asleep with the smile still on my face.

Chapter 6: Creepy Men

Xavier

I'm going to regret this so much, I thought as I got out of the shower and changed. I tiptoed through my room so I wouldn't wake up Sam. I grabbed the pen and a piece of paper and wrote a note to her.

Sam. I had to leave to go do something real quick, but I will be back at noon. Jay and I have a surprise for you and Kyrn, and I think you girls will like it. I'm sorry I wasn't there when you woke up. But I'll be back in about 2 hours.

See you later princess.

Xavier

I left my room and quickly walked down stairs to find Jay eating cereal at the table.

"Hey man," he said while putting a spoonful of cereal in his mouth.

"Hey," I said, grabbing an apple. "Ready to go to the meeting?"

"Yeah. Zander should be here soon," he said looking at his watch.

Right on cue the door opened and in walked Zander, fixing his belt.

"Sorry. I woke up late," he said, focusing on his belt.

Jay and I laughed at him as he struggled with it.

"It's all good dude," I said. "Let's roll."

The meeting was long and all we talked about were the rogues, and checked the status of the pack. That was pretty much it. Nothing really new or special.

We walked up to my house and Ryan, Hunter, and Tim were standing by my door waiting for me.

"Hey, Alpha," they said.

"Hey guys. Okay, so I think I have an idea to get the girls to warm up to us," I said.

"How?" Jay asked skeptically.

"I want you guys," I said pointing to Ryan, Hunter, and Tim, "to take Sam and Kyrn shopping."

"Wait, what?" Tim asked, shocked.

"Do you think that could work?" Jay asked me.

"Yeah. I mean they have been here for a while. Maybe if we let them do this, they won't try to run away..." I paused as I thought about it. "...as much."

"Fine," the guys said.

Jay and I smiled at each other and I opened the door. But what I didn't expect to find was my sexy little mate and Kyrn screaming at the TV. We walked in to see the Vikings playing against the Steelers.

"Come on Vikings!" my sexy mate yelled.

"Pu-lease Sam. Steelers are going to win," Kyrn said smirking.

"Who knew they were football fans." I laughed to Jay and the guys.

***

Sam

Well, Kyrn and I were going try and leave this morning but I saw Hunter and Tim watching football.

And well, it was the Vikings versus the Steelers, so Kyrn and I had to stay.

"Who knew they were football fans." I heard someone laugh.

I turned around and saw Xavier, Jay, Zander, Ryan, Hunter, and Tim standing there watching us in amusement.

I flipped them off and continued watching the game.

"You should have seen them," Hunter said walking over to the couch.

"They were probably going to kill us if we changed the channel. So we did the only smart thing we could do: hand Sam the remote and hide," Tim said laughing.

Zander walked in front of the TV and Kyrn and I both grabbed a pillow and threw it at him.

"Move!" we shouted at the same time.

Zander yelped and ran behind the recliner.

"Remind me when either the Vikings or Steelers are playing, not to go near them," Jay replied laughing. But you could tell he was a little nervous. *Ha ha, good!*

"Go go go!" I yelled as I stood up.

The Vikings scored a touch-down and the score was 49-32.

"Vikings rule! Suck on that, Kyrn!" I yelled, jumping up and down.

I stopped and ran for my life when Kyrn jumped off the couch toward me.

"Ah!" I screamed.

The guys were laughing, but stopped when I pushed them over.

"I'm going to kill you!" Kyrn screamed behind me.

"If you can catch me!" I yelled back at her smirking.

"Don't kill each other," Jay said reaching for Kyrn.

But before that, she managed to grab my shirt and we both fell backwards on the floor. I looked at Kyrn. When we made eye contact, we both started laughing.

Xavier helped me up and looked at me in amusement.

"Okay then," he said smiling. "Anyway, Jay and I decided you girls might like to go shopping."

Kyrn and I looked at him like he was crazy.

"Are you serious?" I asked him.

He nodded and smiled.

Kyrn and I looked at him, then at each other, and then back at him.

"Yes!" we yelled.

The guys groaned and covered their ears.

"Easy there, killers. We have sensitive hearing," Zander mumbled.

"Like a dog," Kyrn and I laughed.

Xavier's eyes popped out of his head and he looked extremely nervous.

"Ha, hah, uh yeah. Like a dog." He laughed nervously.

What's that about?

"But uh...Hunter, Tim, and Ryan are going with you. Jay and I have other stuff to do," Xavier finished as he grabbed Jay's arm.

"Okay," Kyrn and I cried out before running upstairs and getting ready.

When we were, we ran back downstairs and grabbed the guys by their arms, and ran, hauling them outside to their Yukon.

"Shopping!" Kyrn and I yelled.

The ride to the mall wasn't as bad as I thought it was going to be. The guys seemed pretty cool once they started talking and opening up about themselves. So it made the ride seem faster than it actually was. Speaking of which, there is the mall.

We all got out of the vehicle and walked to the store. The minute I stepped foot inside, I saw the store and fell in love.

"Look at those boots!" I yelled running over to this giant wall full of combat boots.

"You know, most girls your age would go for high heels. Not combat boots." Ryan laughed walking up to me.

"Well she's not like most girls. She would rather have nail polish than makeup, hunting than a spa day, and training in martial arts than be afraid to break a nail," Kyrn said looking at me smiling.

"Wow. You aren't like most girls." Ryan said.

"You have no idea." I laughed turning around and trying on the boots.

They were black and the insides camouflage.

"Ooh! Running shoes!" Kyrn yelled running to the other store in front of the one we were at.

"Oh yeah, she loves to go on runs," I said to Ryan.

He sighed, chuckling, as he and Tim ran after her.

I was waiting for the lady to come out and ask for a bigger size but she hadn't come yet. I began softly singing to myself.

"Memories consume
Like opening the wound
I'm picking me apart again
You all assume
I'm safe here in my room
Unless I try to start again
I don't want to be the one
The battles always choose
'Cause inside I realize
That I'm the one confused
I don't know what's worth fighting for
Or why I have to scream.
I don't know why I instigate
And say what I don't mean.
I don't know how I got this way
I know it's not all right.
So I'm breaking the habit,
I'm breaking the habit tonight."

"You have a lovely voice," I heard behind me.

Hunter smiled and sat next to me.

"Thanks. I got it from my mom," I said.

"That's the first time I've ever heard you sing. Why don't you sing more often?"

"I don't know. It's just not something I usually do in front of people."

"How come?"

"I don't know really. When I was little, my mom would take me on stage with her and we would sing in front of the church. We still

49

do it sometimes, but I only feel comfortable singing with her and Kyrn," I said truthfully.

"Oh. Well you have an amazing voice. And good taste in music. I didn't know you liked Linkin Park."

I looked at him in shock and punched his arm. "Just because I'm a girl doesn't mean I listen to shitty music."

He laughed and shook his head.

"So where did they go?" Hunter asked pointing toward their running figures.

"Kyrn saw running shoes in the window. She loves to run," I said. "I don't understand."

"Ah. That makes sense. So, I need to use the little men's room. Can I trust you to stay here and not run off?" he asked, teasing me.

"Are you kidding me? I just want my damn shoes. I've been sitting here waiting for this stupid lady who has yet to make an appearance!" I yelled causing a group of girls to look at me as if I was weird.

"Okay, okay." Hunter laughed shushing me. "Be right back. Stay put."

"I'm not a dog. And don't make me punch you again," I threatened with narrowed eyes as he raised his hands up in defense and walked out of the shoe store.

Where are these freaking ladies? When I find them I'm going to-

"Excuse me," a deep voice said behind me.

I turned around and saw two giant walls. These guys were huge! Like they were tall, buff, and big. One had a scar above his left eye, and the other one had a scar running down his neck.

They were twins, and they scared me. Like, really scare me.

I couldn't help but wonder about these two guys. They gave off this weird, evil vibe thing. And I didn't like it one bit.

"Yes?" I asked him.

"We were wondering if you knew a good place to eat at."

"Sorry, but I'm not from around here."

"Hmm. Interesting." He put his hand on my shoulder and gave it a tight squeeze.

I winced at the pain but didn't say anything.

You never want to show the enemy pain. That's what I was always taught in my martial arts classes. You have to stay strong. I didn't know why I'm referring to him as my enemy, but something just didn't seem right with these two guys.

"Do you know—" he asked, but someone cut him off.

"Sam!" I heard someone call.

Then I was grabbed and thrown behind a tall figure which I now saw was Hunter.

"What are you doing here?" Hunter growled.

Okay, they seriously need to get their throats looked at. I didn't think that's very healthy.

Wait! Why am I caring? They bloody kidnapped Kyrn and me!

"We were just asking this beautiful young lady if she knew a good place to eat," the guy with the neck scar asked.

"Leave!" Hunter yelled.

The twins smirked but nodded and walked out.

When they were gone Hunter grabbed my hand and we hauled ass. Well more he like he did. I was being dragged behind him.

But not before grabbing the rest of my clothes that the guys had bought.

"What's wrong, Hunter?" Ryan asked walking out with Tim and Kyrn carrying shopping bags.

Hunter mumbled setting under his breath and I only heard, "Ogues."

What are ogues?

Kyrn gave me a weird look and I shrugged. I was just as confused as she was.

The guys pulled us toward the door that lead out to the parking lot, and we got in the car. The entire car ride was silent, and every time Kyrn and I asked what was going on, the guys would mumble something about 'I can't believe this is happening,' or 'how did they get here.'

Something along those lines. Who really knows to be honest.

When we arrived back at the house, Zander, Xavier, and Jay looked uneasy. But when their eyes landed on me and Kyrn, they looked relieved. Xavier ran over to me and pulled me into his chest.

I grunted as I made contact with his stone hard chest.

"I'm so glad you're okay," he said hugging me and burying his face in my neck.

"What's going on?" I asked.

"Nothing," Xavier said.

I was seriously so sick of this. I pushed him away and stepped back.

"What was that for?" he asked me, pissed off.

"What. Happened," I demanded.

"Nothing," he said trying to calm down.

"Really? So you're telling me you guys are freaking out because two guys talked to me and you're relieved I'm here safe and sound, and that's nothing?"

"Yes," he said.

His voice was firm and he was trying to convince me.

Well guess what buddy ole pal. It ain't working.

"Bullshit!" I yelled. "You know, I'm really sick of all of this. You guys kidnapped me and Kyrn from my house. Kidnapped! And you won't even tell us why because we 'aren't ready'," I said using air quotes with my fingers. "I'm sick and tired of being lied to, sick and tired of being treated like babies. We can't even look at the front door without being suspected of planning an escape! Like seriously! So what the hell was all that about?"

I was so pissed off at the moment I didn't care if I was yelling.

"Sam, calm down," Hunter said to me.

"Calm down? How would you like it if you were kidnapped from your home and held prisoner and you might not ever be able to see your family again? Huh?" I asked him. He didn't say anything and looked down. "That's what I thought."

I grabbed Kyrn's hand and marched us both toward the house.

"Sam! Wait!" Xavier called after me.

He grabbed my arm and pulled me back toward him.

I yanked my arm out of his grasp.

"Don't touch me," I spat at him.

He looked hurt and I felt a little guilty for yelling at him. I don't know why, though he was the moron that took me.

"Sam. I-I'm sorry," he pleaded.

I closed my eyes because I knew if I looked at his eyes, I would forgive him.

I felt this weird pull every time I was near him and the stupid amazing sparks every time we touched. I felt safe, like he wouldn't hurt me. And that's what scared me the most. I'm scared to trust again. I'm scared that if I trust him, he will end up breaking me, just like Brett did.

"D-don't. Don't touch, o-or even talk to us," I said stepping away from him when I opened my eyes.

His eyes were watering and he looked broken.

Kyrn and I turned around and ran up to the house. We found the room that she stayed in and locked ourselves in it. Looking at each other, we broke down, crying.

"I miss my parents," I said to her.

"Me too," she cried. "Do you think we will ever get to see them again?"

"I don't-" I broke my sentence when I heard a howl in the distance. "Did you hear that?" I asked.

She nodded and we kept on listening.

The howl sounded like he was in pain? He sounded miserable and broken.

How is that even possible?

I shrugged it off and just lay there on the floor with Kyrn crying.

I didn't even know if we would ever get out of there.

Chapter 7: Explain

Sam

We'd been in this room for about three hours.

I didn't know why, but that fight I had with Xavier, it was like my heart broke. And when I saw him like that, saying he was truly sorry, I just didn't know what to do.

"Come on Sam. Let's go for a walk or something," Kyrn said wiping her tears away and standing up.

She held her hand out and I took it reluctantly. I didn't want to leave this room. I just wanted to get swallowed up by a giant black hole and stay there forever.

We quietly made our way downstairs and saw no one in the living room. We checked the kitchen and it was empty too. Kyrn and I looked at each other and shrugged. We checked the clock on the stove; it read 6:27.

"Where is everyone?" I asked. "It's the afternoon."

"I have no idea," she replied. "If we are going for a walk in the woods, do you think we should take some protection? I don't know what's out there."

"The basement," I said remembering all the weapons they had down there, as I made my way over to it. Once down there, we both grabbed some knives and went back upstairs.

We made our way to the door and opened it. We came face first to two very muscular backs.

"Hello ladies," the tall guy said.

"Hi," Kyrn said as we walked around them.

"Wait. You guys can't leave the house, alpha Xavier and beta Jay said so."

"Alpha and beta?" I asked curious.

"Uh never mind that. But you guys can't leave the house."

"We're just going for a walk," I whined.

"I'm sorry but—"

"Listen. Kyrn and I are going for a walk and if you try to stop us again, we will rip your arms off. Okay?" I said to them.

They gulped and stepped out of our way.

"Nice one," Kyrn teased as we made our way to the forest.

"Well. I'm not in the best mood," I laughed.

We stopped at a clearing and sat down. I breathed in the fresh air and looked across the field as the flowers danced in the wind. The tree branches were swaying from the breeze and the air felt nice and cool.

"So what do you think they are hiding from us?" Kyrn asked after a couple minutes of silence.

"I honestly do not know. They keep saying these weird words like alpha and beta. I have never heard those words in my entire life," I mumbled as I raced through my brain trying to figure out what they mean.

"Would you like to know what they mean?" a deep voice said behind us.

Kyrn and I jumped to our feet and turned around to face two men. *Wait just one minute!*

"Hey, it's you guys," I said as I looked at them. It was the guy with the neck scar and the guy with the eye scar.

"You know them?" Kyrn asked.

"Yeah. When we were shopping, they came up to me," I mumbled.

"We should probably introduce ourselves. My name is Michael." Neck-scar guy said. "And that is Leroy," he said pointing to eye-scar guy.

"Okay. I'm Sam, and this is Kyrn," I said.

"Hey," Kyrn said slowly.

Michael and Leroy said hi back and walked toward us. Kyrn and I felt a little uneasy and stepped back. They noticed and stopped walking.

"So. Would you ladies like to know what alpha and beta mean?" Leroy asked with a wink.

"Yes." we said at the same time.

"Freaking Xavier and Jay kidnapped us and they won't tell us why," I mumbled, annoyed.

"You girls are so stupid," Michael said shaking his head.

"Excuse me?" Kyrn said, shocked.

"You are their mates!" Leroy shouted.

"Mates?" I asked them. "Like as in friends? Because if that's what that means then hell, no. We are not their friends."

"They didn't tell you?" He smirked.

"Tell us what?"

"Why tell you when we can show you," he said.

He stepped back and we heard cracks and saw his body morph into a giant wolf.

Wait. How did he turn into a wolf?

"Uh. Kyrn?" I asked, scared.

"You saw that too, right?" she asked me.

"Yeah. I saw that all right."

"Okay good," Kyrn mumbled. "So I'm not going crazy."

"See. This is what Xavier and Jay are hiding from you guys. We are what you call werewolves," Leroy stated, smirking.

Then he too turned into a wolf.

Now standing in front of us were two giant wolves--one a brown wolf, and the other a sand color.

Kyrn and I let out a blood-curdling scream and ran for our lives.

I made it about two steps before I was tackled to the ground. After realizing that I wouldn't be able to turn over, I grabbed the knife that was on my hip.

I gasped as the brown wolf knocked it out of my hands with its paw.

"Kyrn!" I yelled out in fear.

The brown wolf snarled its teeth at me. Suddenly, a midnight blue wolf tackled him to the ground. I watched in shock as the sand colored wolf got tackled by a gray one.

I jumped up, grabbed the knife and put it in the holster, and ran toward Kyrn..

"Are you okay?" she asked me while watching the fight.

"No!" I yelled.

We screamed and shut our eyes.

About a minute later we didn't hear anymore growls or snarls.

I opened one eye to see the blue wolf with the brown wolf in his mouth. He or she, or whatever it was, threw it up against a tree, and looked back at me.

It took a step toward me and I screamed, hugging Kyrn tighter.

It whined and lay down.

"Why isn't it killing us?" Kyrn asked as the gray wolf lay down next to the midnight blue one.

"I don't know. But this is really freaking me out," I said honestly.

The wolves got up and walked toward us. Those gray eyes, they look so familiar.

"Remember what Leroy said. About Jay and Xavier?" I asked all of the sudden.

"Yeah. What about them?" Kyrn asked confused as she held me tighter.

"I think I found them," I said pointing to the wolves walking toward us.

They stopped in front of us and sat down. We heard some cracks and closed our eyes, screaming again. I jumped when I felt hands wrap around my wrists and pull me off the ground.

I still refused to open my eyes.

"Sam. You can open your eyes now," Xavier said sadly.

"You have a lot of explaining to do," I said with my eyes still closed.

I heard Xavier sigh, and then he picked me up, bridal style. "I know, princess."

The walk back seemed to take forever, but before I knew it, we were back at their house.

Xavier took me into his room, while Jay and Kyrn went to Jay's room.

I'd rather be with Kyrn right now, but I guess that isn't happening.

"Okay, so where do you think I should start?" Xavier asked me sitting on the bed.

"The beginning," I told him in a d'uh tone.

"Okay." He sighed again before starting. "There are these things called werewolves. That's what I am. Michael and Leroy are what you called rogues. Rogues are wolves that have been banned, or left their pack. They could have lost their mate, causing them to go crazy and let their wolf have total control over them. A pack is a group of werewolves. Like a family, and everyone in this house is one. I'm what you call an alpha. An alpha is the leader, and I'm the alpha of The Crescent Moon Pack. Jay is my beta or second in command, and Zander is my third in command. Hunter and Tim are guard wolves, bodyguards for example."

"What's a Luna?" I asked. "I heard someone say it."

"A Luna is the alpha's mate. She is equal with the alpha and they run the pack together."

"What's a mate?"

When I brought that up a huge smile spread across his face.

"Do you believe in soul mates?" he asked. I nodded and he smiled again. "A mate is a werewolf's other half. They are the most precious thing a werewolf could ever have. They are your world, nothing else matters. Once you find your mate, all you do is want to protect them," he was speaking with a smile on his face.

"Okay then. I think that's my cue to leave," I said getting up.

"What?" I heard him ask. His hand shot out and grabbed my arm before I made it to the door.

"Dude, you're a freaking werewolf! I'm a human; you guys could like kill me or something!" I said terrified.

58

His eyes grew black and they looked even more terrifying.

"Sam. I would never hurt you! I wouldn't let anyone touch you. You are my mate, my Luna, my everything. I care about you way too much to let someone hurt you," Xavier growled softly.

"No, no, no. I can't be a Luna. I can't help you run this pack, I'm a human. Humans and werewolves don't belong together," I said trying to get away from him.

He noticed me struggling and wrapped his step arms around my waist and held on for dear life.

"Let me go!" I yelled as I started to thrash around.

"No!" he yelled. "Sam, you are mine. And we do belong together. Fate brought us here," he said, smiling.

"I'm not yours okay? I shouldn't even be here. You are the one that kidnapped me!"

"That was because I knew you were my mate. I can't live without you," he shot back.

"No. Just, give me some time to think this all through." He nodded and leaned forward.

I pulled my head away from his and he let it a frustrated sigh.

"Why do you keep pushing me away?" he asked sad and angry.

"I don't know what you are talking about," I defended.

"Why won't you let me kiss you?"

"You are a freaking werewolf! And I barely even know you. Please, just leave," I said.

He growled and stomped toward the door and slammed the door shut.

I sat back on the bed and stared at the wall.

I have a mate. My mate is a werewolf. I'm a Luna.

How the hell does this shit happen?

Chapter 8: I Guess It's Okay

Xavier

"How long are they going to be up there?" I asked pacing back and forth around the living room.

"Just give them time, dude," Zander said.

"Time? They have been up there for two hours. Isn't that long enough?" Jay asked looking sad.

"Not for them. They were nearly killed by rogues, and then you guys decided to tell them the truth after they were almost killed," Zander said.

"Still..." Jay groaned.

"Guys, calm down. They have to come down sooner or later. I can call in re-enforcements," Zander said smiling.

"Who?" I asked suspiciously.

"Chloe. She can talk to them, since she is a girl. Girls always listen to each other's advice and opinions more."

"You got a point there. Call her!" I said urgently.

"Okay, okay. Calm down dude. Geez," Zander said getting up and getting his phone out.

"Those stupid rogues ruined everything!" Jay yelled throwing a chair into the wall.

"I know!" I groaned kicking the table over. "My mate is terrified of me. She shouldn't be! She won't even talk to me." I sat down with my head in my hands.

"Well you guys need to calm down. Throwing and kicking shit over isn't going to help make them less scared of you two," Ryan said as he picked up the chair and fixed the table. "Zander is going to call Chloe and she'll talk to your mates."

"You think?" Jay asked him.

Ryan nodded and Zander walked back in.

"She's on her way. She'll be here in about an hour since she was heading over here anyway. She finally finished school, so she will be staying in this house," Zander said, and I nodded.

I looked at the stairs debating if I should walk up there or not.

"Come on. Let's watch TV. Remember, they have to come down sooner or later. And besides, you have guards standing under their windows." I reluctantly nodded and sat down in the couch with Zander, Jay, Ryan, Hunter, and Tim.

Please, forgive me Sam.

***

Sam

Kyrn and I locked ourselves in a guest room while everyone else was downstairs.

"I'm so hungry," Kyrn whined.

"Me too," I said.

My stomach decided to make an appearance and sound like a dying whale.

I groaned and held my stomach. We lay there groaning for about another hour or so before Kyrn spoke up.

"I need food in me," Kyrn said while her stomach was growling too.

"I'm not going downstairs with those things," I defended.

"I don't know. I'm starting to think it might be worth it so I can get food." She laughed.

"They could kill us!" I said.

"Wait a minute." She paused and patted her ankle before giving me a giant grin. "We have our knives."

She pulled up her pants legs with a smirk.

I quickly patted my ankles and lifted my pants legs to see my knives.

"Yes!" I said grabbing them. "Let's go."

We grabbed our knives and unlocked the door, looking both ways to make sure the coast was clear. Then we quietly made our way downstairs to the kitchen.

"There's the kitchen," Kyrn whispered.

"Almost there," I said tiptoeing.

"Sam?" A deep voice said behind me.

I screamed bloody murder and chucked the knife at whoever was behind me. I turned around so fast I almost lost my balance.

"What the hell was that for?" screamed Xavier, who was panting and sprawled out across the floor.

I squeaked and jumped back again. "You scared me!"

"Okay I'm sorry, but you didn't have to throw a bloody knife at my head!" He yelled, standing up and pointing at the knife embedded in the wall. He walked over to it and took it out of the wall.

My weapon!

"Hey. Give that back!" I yelled.

"No. Why do you even have a knife?" Xavier asked as he held it in his hand.

"For protection, you moron. Now give it back!" I whined.

"No. You don't need protection from me, Sam. I'm not going to hurt you," he said taking a few steps toward me.

I grabbed the other knife and held it out in front of me.

He put his hands up and sighed.

"Stay. Back," I said.

Kyrn pulled her knife out and stood next to me.

"What happened? I heard someone scream," Jay said walking in here. His face paled when he saw the knives in our hands. "Why do they have knives?"

"They are for 'protection'," Xavier said using air quotes. "Even though we won't hurt them!" He exaggerated to us.

62

I rolled my eyes and sneered. "How do we know that? You guys can kill us whenever you want. You freaking turn into wolves! And you kidnapped us!"

"Oh my gosh. Quit being so over dramatic. We could never hurt you guys. You are our mates. And Sam, you are our Luna. They *can't* hurt you. And Kyrn, you are our beta female. We can't hurt you either," Xavier explained.

"You kept this secret from us!" I yelled, hurt.

"I know, and I'm sorry. I didn't want you to be afraid of me," he pleaded.

I wanted to believe him, I really did. I guess I was just a little scared and I was falling for him. A werewolf kidnapper. I guess this mate thing is true.

I was snapped out of my thoughts when I noticed Xavier reach for me. I screamed and ran past him and toward the door.

"Shit," I heard him mumble and chase after me.

When I got to the door I flung it open and almost hit some girl standing there. I really didn't care at the moment; I was too busy running from Xavier.

She had short blonde hair and bright blue eyes that sparkled.

"Hey Chloe," Xavier said as he caught up to me.

"Hello? Why is there a girl hiding behind me?" She asked crossing her arms over her chest and tapping her foot impatiently.

"He kidnapped me and my friend!" I yelled.

"You *what*?" This Chloe chick yelled in disbelief.

"She's my mate!" Xavier defended. "So technically, it's not considered kidnapping."

"Yes, it is!" Chloe and I yelled.

Xavier sighed and looked at the ground.

"Wait, does she know?" Chloe asked carefully.

"Yes. Leroy and Michael made sure of it," Xavier growled out.

Chloe quickly turned around and pulled me in a hug.

"Oh my gosh. I am so sorry you had to find out that way," she said quietly.

"Wait, you're one too?" I asked pushing her away.

She noticed my fear and gave a small nod. "Yes. And I truly am sorry you had to find out this way. And I'm sorry for Xavier's stupid behavior." She turned to him. "I mean, seriously? You kidnapped her? You could have had a better method. Like, get to know her first," she scolded him.

He looked guilty.

"You're not so bad you know? Even if you are a werewolf. You made him feel bad," I laughed.

Xavier glared at me before turning around and walking away.

"Come on. Let's get you back inside and get you some food. I can hear your stomach growl," she teased.

I blushed and nodded.

"Sam!" I heard Kyrn yell.

I ran into the kitchen and saw her behind the counter, and Jay on the other side.

"I'm not going to hurt you Kyrn. I couldn't," Jay said pleading.

"Let me guess. You kidnapped her?" Chloe asked, pissed.

"Uh. Maybe?" Jay said quietly.

"Yes!" Kyrn yelled and ran over to me when he wasn't paying attention.

"I can't believe you guys. Kidnapping your mates?" Chloe glared at them.

"Hey, babe," Zander said walking up to Chloe and kissing her.

"Oh yeah, he helped," I said crossing my arms.

"Zander?" Chloe warned.

Zander's face paled and he gave me a death glare.

I smirked and flipped him off. "That's what you get."

"Alpha's order!" he accused suddenly pointing at Xavier.

"But....that's.... But," Xavier groaned sinking into the recliner.

"How do you know them?" I asked suddenly curious.

"Zander's my mate," she said pointing at him while he gave us a wide smile. "Xavier's the alpha, and Jay is my stupid moron of a brother."

"Oh gosh. I am so sorry," I said putting a hand on her shoulder.

"Why?" she asked me, laughing.

"You have to live with them."

She smiled in amusement then faked a sob. "I know. It's so hard."

Kyrn and I laughed while the guys scoffed.

"Seriously. You should see them in the mornings sometimes, they are like…" She paused and used a deep voice. "Roar! I'm hungry. Roar! I will kill you all if you wake me up. Roar—don't disobey my order. Well, that last one was for Xavier." She smiled.

Kyrn and I broke out into a fit of giggling and Xavier rolled his eyes.

"We do not 'say' roar. We do actually growl," Xavier said proudly as he nodded his head.

"You whine too much," I said laughing.

"Ha hah, funny." He scowled some more.

"I think you guys owe the ladies an apology. That means all of you! Even you, Ryan, Hunter, Tim," Chloe said sternly.

The guys groaned but nodded.

"We are sorry," they mumbled.

"What was that? I don't think they heard you," Chloe said cupping her ear.

"We're sorry," they said a little bit louder.

"What?" Kyrn and I asked.

"We. Are. Sorry," they yelled.

We nodded and smiled in amusement.

"Does this mean you will give us a chance?" Xavier asked us cautiously and quietly

Kyrn and I looked at each other before taking a deep breath and letting it out. *I can't believe I'm doing this.*

"We guess," I said for us.

Xavier gave me a huge grin and ran toward me lifting me up in his arms. I let out a yelp of surprise and he put his face in the crook of my neck.

"Thank you, thank you, thank you," he said over and over again.

"You're welcome. Maybe this won't be so bad; it's like a personal Taylor Lautner." I smiled.

"Oh. he's so hot," Kyrn said and Chloe nodded.

"Hell yeah, he is," I said laughing.

I heard Xavier growl and he pulled back.

"Excuse me?" he asked.

Zander and Jay both had their arms crossed, and looked at the girls.

"Yeah I probably should have mentioned this, but mates are extremely jealous. And it's worse because he's an alpha," Chloe said apologetically.

"Oh-h," I drew it out.

"Yeah. 'Oh-h'," Xavier said before holding into me tighter.

"Ah. Can't...breathe. Let...go," I wheezed.

"Oh, sorry princess," Xavier gave me a small smile and set me down. "It's just I'm happy. I finally got my mate and she accepts me."

I blushed and looked down at the tiled floor.

"Uh, yeah," I said.

"Come on Sam. We should probably go to bed now."

"But I'm not tired," I said. And of freaking course I let out a small yawn.

"I beg to differ." He smirked.

I sighed and nodded in defeat.

"Fine. Night guys. Night Kyrn and Chloe."

"Night Sam," Kyrn said before being dragged up the stairs by Jay.

"You, Kyrn, and I are hanging out tomorrow," Chloe said determined.

"But I just got her to accept me," Xavier whined.

"Yeah. But I just met her and Kyrn. You can deal with it," she said walking out, leaving no room to argue.

I laughed and Xavier looked down at me and smiled.

"Come on." He tugged on my arm and we went upstairs to his room. But I quickly grabbed an apple before we left the kitchen.

I walked into the bathroom and changed. After I finished my apple, I brushed my teeth and walked back out to see Xavier in nothing but boxers watching football. My eyes raked over his face and down his chest to his abs.

Oh my gosh. His body was so fit, tan, gorgeous, perfect, delicious-

"You okay?" Xavier asked, with amusement in his voice.

"What? Oh yeah," I said playing it cool and clearing my throat. "Uh. I'm good."

"You don't have to be embarrassed, princess." He chuckled.

"I-I don't know what y-you're talking about."

"Ri-i-ighht." He laughed and pulled me so my back was flush against his naked, rock hard chest.

I shivered, but not in the bad way. *What's happening to me?*

He turned my head so I was looking at him and leaned in. My eyes widened in shock and I turned my head sharply.

"Why do you keep pushing me away?" he growled in frustration.

"N-no reason," I rushed out and tried to turn back around but he wouldn't budge.

"Do you not trust me?"

"I-I don't know," I stuttered as I refused to look at him.

I did trust him honestly. It just scared me to think that. I don't quite fully understand the feelings I have for him, and I don't understand how they got formed. But they did, and it was truly scaring me.

"Who made you put up your walls? "he demanded.

"No one."

"Sam, someone has hurt you!"

"Just drop it. It's over and done with. I'm not getting back with Brett anytime soon," I said getting pissed.

"Who the hell is Brett?" Xavier's voice boomed.

I cringed back in fear and slapped a hand over my mouth.

Shit, shit, shit.

Chapter 9: What's The Mating Process

Sam

"Oh. Umm, well. He's just a guy. So I'm going to go to sleep now," I rushed out and turned around in the bed.

He growled and turned me back around. *Come on! Can I ever catch a break?*

"Who. Is. Brett," he growled.

"No one, okay?"

"Sam?"

"Listen. Can we please talk about this another time? I don't really want to talk about him," I replied, looking down at my hands.

He sighed, and finally nodded. "Fine. But you are telling me about him tomorrow," Xavier mumbled.

"Okay," I groaned in defeat and closed my eyes. I want sleep now.

I blinked my eyes open a couple of times and the chill hit me. I shivered and wrapped the blankets around me tighter, and moved closer to where Xavier was lying. When I felt nothing I reopened my eyes and saw he wasn't there.

I got out of bed moments later and went to the bathroom to get ready. After my shower and brushing my teeth and hair, I walked downstairs to get breakfast.

"Hey Hunter, hey Tim," I said grabbing a bowl.

"Hey Luna," they replied.

"Oh gosh, no. Please, call me Sam. I'm still not used to this whole Luna, alpha shit." I laughed.

They chuckled and nodded.

"Hey guys. Luna," Ryan said walking into the kitchen.

"Please, call me Sam," I begged.

"All right, Sam." He smiled.

I nodded and grabbed frosted flakes. Yum!

"So. Where's Kyrn?" I asked.

"I don't really know. Sleeping maybe?" Tim said shrugging.

"Aren't you guys supposed to be guarding us?" I questioned with a smirk.

Tim groaned and walked up the steps to go wake her up.

"Wait for it…" I smiled.

"Wait for wha-?" Hunter was cut off by screaming.

"What the hell is your problem? It's eight in the fucking morning on a Sunday! I want to sleep!" The yelling stopped and was followed by a loud thud and a yelp.

I smiled when I heard heavy footsteps running down the steps.

"Word of advice. Don't wake Kyrn up in the mornings," Tim said holding his cheek.

I busted out laughing and bent over the table holding my stomach.

"Sam? Are you okay?" I heard a deep voice yell.

I looked up through the laughter tears and saw Xavier leaning over me. I nodded and straightened up.

"Tim woke Kyrn up," I said calming down.

"Is that bad?" he asked me confused.

I nodded and took Tim's face in between my hands and looked at his cheek. There was a red handprint.

"Is it noticeable?" Tim asked me.

"Yeah," they all said.

"What happened?" Jay asked.

"Tim woke Kyrn up. And she doesn't like being woken up early. Believe me. I would know," I said rubbing my face.

Everyone made an 'oh' sound and nodded in understanding.

Kyrn came down dressed and went straight for the food. Shocker.

"Hey sleeping beauty," I joked.

She flipped me off and turned back to the refrigerator.

"So. Are you going to tell me about Brett now?" Xavier said crossing his arms over his chest.

Kyrn stiffened and looked at me wide eyed.

I think Jay noticed because he turned to Kyrn. "Do you know Brett Kyrn?"

"Uh. No?" she said unsure of what to say.

"Girls..." they said.

Come on! A distraction would be really nice right about now.

"Ready girls?" Chloe asked as she walked into the kitchen with a smile.

Thank you Chloe. I owe you one. Kyrn and I visibly relaxed and nodded eagerly.

We ran to where she was and grabbed one of her arms and pulled her outside to the Yukon. We heard growls and ran faster.

"Whoa. What are you girls running from? I thought you were cool with us being werewolves," she said as she got in the driver's seat. She kind of sounded a little hurt.

"No. no. no. We are, trust me. It's just, last night I might have said something about an ex-boyfriend. And I wasn't really ready to talk about him yet," I said buckling my seatbelt.

"Oh. What happened?" she asked quietly while pulling out of the driveway.

"If I tell her, you have to tell her about Trey," I said pointing to Kyrn.

She hesitantly nodded, so we told her everything about Brett and Trey, from the day we met them till now.

"Oh my gosh. What an ass! Like, seriously. You got hit." She pointed to Kyrn. "And yours was an extremely jealous asshole!"

"Eyes on the road!" I screamed. She laughed and I sighed in relief that we didn't die. "I know. We didn't realize they were like that. I guess I just liked having someone around me all the time and I didn't really care how they acted."

"It was nice having someone around. But when Sam came to my house with the split lip and black eye, I started to realize he was a

70

jerk," she said playing with her shirt. She always did that when she was nervous or scared.

I always bite my lip whenever I'm nervous or scared.

"Oh. I know how you guys feel. Ex-boyfriends are a pain." She laughed trying to lighten the mood.

"Yeah. And thank you for saving us from them in the kitchen earlier," I said.

Kyrn nodded and smiled.

"Anytime. That's what girlfriends are for." She smiled and patted my shoulder.

"So. What mall are we going to?" I asked as the mall was in site.

"There's one in town. I want to go to Kohl's." Chloe smiled.

I nodded. "Okay. We can help you pick stuff out. Kyrn and I already went shopping a couple days ago."

After walking around with Chloe, I've come to accept that she is freaking awesome. I love her. She's really nice and cool to talk to. It's easy to relate to her. She's pretty funny as well.

Because we were having so much fun, the time at the mall seemed very short.

"Ready, ladies?" Chloe asked.

"Yes," Kyrn and I said together.

We put the shopping bags in the trunk and headed back to the house.

We spent the entire time belting out the words to all of the songs we loved. It was a very entertaining ride, and we got many weird looks from the people we passed. We even had guys whistle and wink at us.

It was quite disturbing if you ask me.

We arrived at the house and Xavier, Zander, and Jay looked stressed.

"Come help get the bags out, guys," Chloe said.

"Do you have any idea what time it is?" Zander yelled.

"Um, six?" Chloe shrugged.

"You guys could have been hurt," Xavier said walking up to us.

"We didn't. We were fine," I tried to calm him down but he was really worried. "Xavier? Are you okay?"

His eyes darkened. What is that?

"Uh. Y-yeah. I'm f-fine," he stuttered as he walked inside and shut the door.

"Okay then? What was the about?" I asked Chloe.

"Let's just say, he has a horny wolf. And it's like a hundred times worse because he's a guy and he's an alpha."

"Oh gross!" I yelled covering my ears.

"Trust me, you won't be saying that for long. You're going to love it. It's all part of the mating process." She smiled.

"My poor ears!" I yelled again. "Wait. What's the mating process?"

"The guy bites the girl's neck and then they have sex after it pretty much," she said causally.

"Whoa, whoa, whoa. He does what to my neck?" I shrieked.

"Bites it."

"Oh, hell no!" Kyrn and I said simultaneously.

Chapter 10: How About No

**

Sam

"He has to," Chloe said looking at us weirdly.

"Uh why?" Kyrn asked shocked.

"A bite mark tells other males that you are taken and your mate's scent gets mixed in with yours. Then to complete the mating process, you guys have sex. Then your mate's scent is completely mixed in with yours. And then 'tada!' Completely mated!" she squealed the last, with a smile.

I shook my head back and forth. "Again, hell no!"

She seemed taken aback by this. "Why not?"

"I'm only eighteen. I'm not going to have sex with my kidnapper and he isn't going to bite my neck. That's just weird!"

"What's weird?" Xavier asked walking back with Jay.

"Oh this oughta be good," Zander said crossing his arms.

"I wonder how they will take it," Ryan said with amusement.

"Who will take what?" Jay asked us, honestly confused.

"Well. Kyrn and Sam don't want you guys to bite them, and they don't want to have sex with you either," Chloe said walking over to where Zander and Ryan are.

Xavier's and Jay's head snapped toward us, and I think their eyes got darker.

"Why not?" Xavier asked through gritted teeth.

I flinched at the sudden anger in his voice and took a step back. Even if he is my mate and he swore to not hurt me, he still scares me.

"Uh. I-I." Fear was taking over and I couldn't finish my sentence.

I think he noticed, because his eyes went back to normal and his features softened. He walked up to me and pulled me into a hug.

"I'm sorry I got mad. I understand if you don't want us," he said and his arms pulled me in tighter before he let go. I saw a tear slip out and he looked toward the ground while walking away.

"What? No!" I yelled and jumped on his back so he would stop walking.

I don't know why I'm acting like this. It must be that weird mate thingy. It's still weird to me. I'm falling for my werewolf kidnapper mate. Yeah, that doesn't sound weird at all.

"But you said-" He started talking but I clamped my hand over his mouth.

"Xavier. Shut up and let me talk." I giggled.

I felt him nod so I took my hand off his mouth and slid down his back.

"Listen. I'm not rejecting you Xavier. I don't know why, but I have got extremely strong feelings for you. I have no idea where they came from, but I know they are there. It's probably this mate pull thing and it's kind of scaring me to like you, but I'm not rejecting you. I only said that because I'm eighteen, and I'm not ready to have sex yet. And besides, if you went up to some random person and were like 'hey, I'm going to bite your neck so other males know you are mine. Don't freak out or anything', they probably would freak out. It's weird." I laughed at the end.

"So you're not rejecting me?" he asked me slowly. I smiled and shook my head. A flood of relief washed across his face and he picked me up. "Oh, thank God. I don't know what I would have done of you did reject me."

"Mates are that important to you guys?"

"You have no idea, princess." He chuckled.

I hugged him back and he finally set me back on the ground.

"So what happens if someone rejects you?" I asked curiously.

He gives me a sad look.

"There really isn't a point to live. Mates are your everything. They are the reason you breathe, wake up, everything you do, they are the reason. You become hallow and depressed and don't want to live on," Xavier explained as he looked me in the eye.

I gasped. "Oh wow." That sounds awful. I don't know what I would do if I lost Xavier. *Wow, I sound like one of those crazy clingy ex-girlfriends.*

"Yeah. It's not good. That's why if you rejected me, I would probably lock you up in a tower or something so I would know you are okay, and I could visit you whenever I wanted." He shrugged and walked back inside.

I looked at his retreating figure and my mouth fell wide open.

"He's just joking," I paused and looked at Chloe. "Right? He seriously wouldn't lock me up in a tower, right?"

She gave me a small smile. "I'm afraid he's not joking. He probably honestly would do that."

"Wait, what?"

"I'm serious. He's an alpha and a guy. The possessiveness and protectiveness are going to be, like, ten times more effective than just a regular werewolf."

"Oh, lord."

"You're in for a wild ride, Sam."

"I can tell." I laughed.

We talked for a little bit longer until we reached the house.

"Don't worry. She'll give in and let me eventually," I heard Xavier say.

"Hopefully mine will too," Jay said.

What are they talking about?

We walked inside and saw the guys at the table.

"What were you guys talking about?" Chloe asked them.

Xavier and Jay smiled mischievously but shrugged and turned toward each other again.

"Please, tell us," Kyrn said hugging Jay from behind.

Jay stiffened and closed his eyes breathing hard.

'Keep it up,' I mouthed to her.

She winked, and turned back to him. She kissed the back of his neck, and Jay's hands gripped the island tightly. It looked like the island was about to break.

"Please Jay," Kyrn pushed on.

"We were talking about how you girls are going to want us to bite you and claim you," he rushed out.

Kyrn smirked and walked over to me.

"Is that so?" I asked, crossing my arms.

"Traitor," Xavier mumbled to Jay.

"Huh. You have your mate do that to you, and tell me you can resist," he defended.

"You're whipped already," Xavier teased.

"You are too."

"Am not."

Jay looked at me and I nodded. I walked up to Xavier and he looked at me curiously. I hoped I could do this. Kyrn was always better at doing this stuff. But I've picked up on some stuff, so hopefully this will work.

Fingers crossed!

"What did you say about it?" I asked him while wrapping my arms around his waist.

"Nothing," he said.

I stood up on my tippy-toes and kissed him between his shoulder blades. He was too tall and it was easier for Kyrn because Jay was sitting down.

He sucked in a breath and I chuckled.

"Please," I pressed on while putting my hands on his abs. This damn shirt is in the way, and I would really like it if it was off so I could— *Oh my gosh. Bad Sam, bad. Get your mind out of the gutter. Bad girl.*

"I-I," his voice trailed off when I started moving my hands around his stomach and chest.

"You...?" I questioned. This is so much fun, I laughed to myself.

"I said we could get you guys to want us and claim you," he strained out.

I nodded and walked back over to Kyrn and Chloe. Zander and Ryan went to the fridge. *Big shocker there.*

"You were saying?" Jay smirked and laughed.

"Oh, shut up," Xavier growled. "But it's going to happen." He smiled at us.

Kyrn and I laughed. "How about 'no'."

"How about yes," Xavier said grabbing a water bottle.

"Whatever helps you guys to sleep at night," I replied.

"It's going to happen."

"No, it's not," I said smiling at him. "Oh, Kyrn, Chloe and I are out."

"But we have to talk," Xavier said with a frown. "And besides, you just went out."

"We can talk when we get back."

"But—"

"Please. Come on." I gave him the puppy dog face.

"Fine," he groaned and reluctantly nodded.

"Yay!" I shouted. I ran to him and gave him a peck on the cheek and a hug before the girls and I ran out to the car.

"Let's do this!" Kyrn shouted.

"Wait!" We heard behind us.

We turned around and saw Tim and Hunter running toward us. "We have to come with you. Alpha's and Beta's orders," Hunter said.

"They owe us big time," Tim mumbled.

"Yeah, yeah, let's go!" I shouted, and we jumped in the car.

Chapter 11: Run-ins

Sam

Kyrn, Chloe, Hunter, Tim, and I arrived at Subway quickly because some people—Hunter and Tim—were complaining about being hungry.

They showed me and Kyrn around town. There was a movie theater, a mall, restaurants like Olive Garden, Steak 'n Shake, and many, many others.

So here we were sitting in Subway eating our sandwiches. Mine included Italian bread, cold cut, bacon, lettuce, mayo, cheese, and pickles. I loved bacon. It was my weakness. That and Oreos!

The bell dinged and I heard a voice all too familiar. "I'm so in the mood for some Subway."

Kyrn looked up and stiffened along with me.

"Oh no," I said out loud.

"It's both of them!" she said in disbelief.

I turned around and there they were. Brett and Trey.

"Shit," I mumbled.

Since Hunter was sitting next to me and he was on the outside, I ducked down and used his body as a shield. Kyrn saw what I did, and moved and hid behind Tim.

They looked confused.

"Are you guys okay?" Chloe asked us.

"Yeah, we are fine," Kyrn said quietly.

"Then why are you girls hiding?" Tim asked.

"Just stay right here, please," I said uneasily.

"Luna. What's wrong?" Hunter asked in full protective mode.

I groaned as he called me Luna. Oh well, better get used to him calling me that when he needs to. I sighed and decided to tell them.

"My and Kyrn's old boyfriends are right there. I caught mine having sex with another girl in his room on our two-year anniversary. Kyrn's was a complete ass and was abusive. He would yell at her and sometimes hit her for stupid reasons. He also punched me when I confronted him about hitting her. His name is Trey." I pointed to him and they looked. "My ex is Brett." And I pointed to him. "Brett didn't hit me but he got extremely jealous and would get in my face and yell at me. But some of the time he got really close to hitting me but he never did." I looked down and bit my lip while Kyrn was playing with her hands.

Hunter, Tim, and Chloe all looked at us in shock, disbelief anger, and sorrow—and growled lowly.

Tim growled, grabbing his drink. "I'll throw everything away, then we can get out of here."

We nodded and Hunter scooted closer to me and put his arm in front of my waist under the table for protection. I smiled a thank you and he gave me a smile back.

"Ready?" Chloe asked.

I nodded frantically.

Hunter slowly got up so I still could be hidden behind him.

"Sam?" I heard Brett's voice.

"Crap," I muttered.

"Is that you?" I heard footsteps and someone put their hand on my arm and turned me around. "Hey." Brett said smiling.

"Kyrn," I heard Trey's voice.

Anger bubbled up inside me when I saw him touching her shoulder. I yanked my arm free from Brett's grasp and marched over to Trey.

"Oh hey Sa—" He never finished because I pulled my arm back and socked him in the jaw.

"Don't ever. And I mean ever, touch Kyrn again. Got it?" I spat at him while he was on the ground holding his jaw.

He glared at me and I smiled sweetly before I grabbed Kyrn's hand and walked over to Hunter, Tim, and Chloe who were smiling proudly at me.

"What?" I asked laughing.

"Nice punch," Tim complimented.

"Thanks." I smiled with a wink.

"Sam, wait," Brett yelled running up to me.

Hunter stepped in the way and Brett came to a halt.

"Don't even," Hunter said with a glare.

"Could you please move so I can get to my girlfriend?" Brett said bitterly.

I gasped in surprise. "You have the nerve to call me your girlfriend? After what you did to me? Should I remind you? Probably. You had sex with another girl on our two-year anniversary."

"I know. And I'm sorry, I was so stupid to do that. Please, I regret it so much. I love you so much, Sam. I'm sorry I took you for granted. I miss you, I miss holding you, I miss kissing you, and I miss seeing your smile and knowing I'm the reason," Brett rambled.

"Please. You were barely the reason. Kyrn was the main reason. You got jealous even if a guy walked right past me," I spat.

"I was afraid someone better was going steal your heart."

I scoffed. "You cussed out a waiter for talking to me. And he was taking my order because that's his job!"

He looked up at me and anger showed. "Oh my gosh. You are so overly dramatic!" he yelled.

And there's his anger problem I know and love. Ha ha...sarcasm right there.

"He was flirting with you and I'm your boyfriend. Only I can do that. Gosh, get the damn story right Sam, and quit lying to everyone. You were always good at lying." Brett yelled as he threw his hands up in the air

"I think we need to leave," Hunter said grabbing my frozen hand.

I can't believe Brett just said that.

"No you don't. Trey and I need to have our girls back before you leave. So if you could give us Kyrn and Sam, then you guys can leave," Brett said.

I looked over at Trey and he was burning holes in my head. I smirked when I saw his jaw was slightly crooked. I think I broke it. Oops?

"I don't think so." Hunter chuckled.

"And why not?" Brett spat.

Hunter smirked. "Because if you took Sam and Kyrn away, then alph— Um Xavier and Jay wouldn't be very happy. And when they aren't happy, well let's just say it's not a pretty sight, and you don't want to be the cause of their anger."

"Who the hell are Xavier and Jay?"

"Their boyfriends," Tim answered.

Both Trey and Brett stood there in shock before their faces turned angry. And a lot of anger might I add.

"And we have to go meet them. Bye," Hunter added.

"Whatever. But we'll get them back! Just wait and see," he turned to me and Kyrn and gave us an evil smile. "And that's a promise." With that, he and Trey walked out the door.

I grabbed Kyrn's hand and ran out of Subway.

"Let's go home guys," Chloe said full of anger.

The car ride felt longer than normal, and I just wanted to be with Xavier right now. I felt protected with him.

"Hey," Kyrn said as she nudged me softly. "We're back at the house."

I slowly looked up at her and nodded. "Right."

"It's going to be okay, Sam," Kyrn offered a small smile.

I returned a small smile and hopped out of the car, running to go find Xavier. I just wanted to be in his arms because I felt so safe. I wonder if it's this mate thing.

"Hey. How was—" I cut him off by jumping in his arms. "Miss me that much?" he asked amused.

Tears made their way down my face and I held onto him tighter.

"Princess, what's wrong?" Xavier asked worried.

"Let's just say we ran into their ex boyfriends," Chloe spat with disgust.

Xavier growled loudly and held me tighter. "What ex boyfriends?" he asked through gritted teeth.

"Brett and Trey," she said. "But it was kind of awesome becau—"

"How was it awesome?" Jay yelled.

"She punched Trey in the jaw—and I think she broke it." Chloe laughed.

"Really?" Jay asked me.

I turned around in Xavier's arms and nodded.

"He grabbed Kyrn's shoulder," Chloe said as she shuddered in disgust.

"He did what? No other man is allowed to touch Kyrn besides me!" he growled out.

"It's okay. I think he got the message when Sam punched him," she said smiling.

"Good job, princess," Xavier laughed.

"Thank you," I giggled. Xavier smiled, but then turned very serious, and stood me down.

"You need to tell us everything that happened," he said crossing his arms over his chest. "And I mean everything, straight from the beginning until now."

I sighed, and reluctantly nodded. I told them about Brett and Trey. How they acted, how we all met, and how they are related.

"And that's all of it," I said to him and Jay.

I finally told Xavier and Jay the story between me and Kyrn and our exes. It 'only' took about thirty minutes to explain, because they kept growling, and interrupting us every now and then.

When I looked up from my shaking hands, Xavier looked like he was about to kill someone. Same with Jay. Both of their eyes were glowing, and it was starting to creep me out. But, those glowing stormy grey eyes were amazing. I needed to stop looking, because I was starting to get lost in them.

Suddenly his eyes snapped to me and a growl rumbled through his chest.

"Uh, Xavier?" I asked.

"He can't do that! And he isn't getting you!" His voice was deep and full of power.

That doesn't sound like him.

"Um Jay?" I asked him, worriedly.

"You need to calm him down, Sam. His wolf is trying to take over, and he is going into full protective mode," he answered wrapping his arms around Kyrn's waist and pulling her behind him.

"You just said his wolf's taken over. I'm not going near him," I said scooting away from Xavier, or from his wolf.

He growled and stood up walking over to me.

My eyes went big but I couldn't move. I was frozen to my spot.

"Calm down, Ryder," Jay said urgent. "Sam."

"Who's Ryder?" I asked him, completely confused.

"Me," Xavier or his wolf said.

"Um, I thought you were Xavier."

"I'm his wolf." Ryder smiled at me.

"Oh," was all I could say.

Ryder got close to me and I scooted away still terrified. He growled and scooped me up in his arms.

"Hey. Put me down!" I shouted.

"No. I will not have you taken away from me. You belong to me," Xavier, or I guess Ryder, said.

"I belong to myself. I'm not an object you know," I said as I folded my arms over my chest.

"I know you aren't, princess. But you being my mate means you do belong to me just as I belong to you." Ryder smiled.

"This is so weird."

"I know." He chuckled.

"Can you put me down now?"

"No. I like having you in my arms," he said while putting his face in my neck and sniffing. *Did he just sniff me? Seriously?*

"Yeah. And I like having my feet on the ground," I mumbled as I tried to touch the ground beneath my feet.

He shook his head and wrapped my legs around his waist and put his hand right under my butt.

"Oh great. You're a pervert, too." I sighed.

Both Kyrn and Jay held in a laugh and had to cover it with a cough.

But Ryder on the other hand, he didn't laugh. He growled. "I'm not a pervert Sam. You're my mate; I'm allowed to touch you," he replied while holding onto me tighter.

"You men are so hard to understand," I stated wiggling out of his grasp. He set me back down and closed his eyes.

When he opened them again, they were back to normal, not glowing with grey color.

"Well, you women are just as hard to understand," he defended.

"Whatever. I'm going to bed," I said walking up the steps.

"Okay. Let's go. Night everyone," Xavier yelled while walking up the steps.

I still have a lot of questions to ask him.

Like why he sniffed me, why his eyes changed color, and what it means when his wolf is out? I can always ask him in the morning.

Chapter 12: Horny Wolves

Sam

"Good morning everyone." I yawned while walking into the kitchen.

"Good morning," they replied back.

"Hey princess," Xavier whispered while giving me a hug.

I laughed and hugged him back.

"So, I was thinking," Chloe said smiling.

"You? Think? Shocker!" Jay hooted.

Chloe gaped at him and everyone was trying to hold in a laugh. "I'm going to ignore that comment. Any hoo, for breakfast I'm taking you and Kyrn and we're going into town. So go get ready."

Kyrn and I nodded eagerly and ran upstairs. We ran back down stairs ready to go in fifteen minutes. New record for Kyrn. She. Takes. Forever! Believe me.

"Ready!" we both yelled.

"What about us?" Jay asked pointing to himself, Xavier, Zander, and Ryan.

Chloe shrugged. "Go find something to do. Girls day."

With that we ran outside and into the Yukon.

"Girls day!" we all yelled.

We spent the entire time jamming out to the Backstreet Boys. Chloe had their albums on her phone. Looks like its throwback Thursday!

"Starbucks!" I yelled, jumping out of the car and running inside

"Is she always like this?" I heard Chloe ask as she and Kyrn came up next to me.

"You have no idea. If she could marry Starbucks, she would."

We ordered our drinks and sat at a table waiting for our coffee and Kyrn's hot chocolate. She doesn't like coffee. I think something is wrong with her.

"Here you are, ladies." A blonde boy with bright green eyes came over and gave us our drinks. "Hi. I'm Tucker," he said smiling at me.

"Hey. I'm Sam," I replied.

He took my hand and kissed it.

"A lovely name for a lovely girl," Tucker winked.

I blushed a little and giggled.

Chloe cleared her throat. "Sorry dude. She's taken."

"I am?"

"She is?" Tucker asked, just as confused as I am.

"Yes. Now if you will please move along. That would be great," she said rather rudely to him.

He looked at me and I shrugged. He winked at me and walked away.

"Chloe, what was all that about?" I asked her.

"He was flirting with you," she simply stated.

"He was just being friendly."

"Sam. You need to understand this. Xavier is your mate which means no other boys. That means You Are Taken."

"I'm not taken," I said, confused.

"Yes you are," Chloe argued.

"He never officially asked me out. So until then, I'm still single."

"Try telling him that." She chuckled.

"Well we humans have different ways of being together than you werewolves have. We humans need to be asked out in order for us to be taken. So once he asks me out, then I'm taken," I finished with a proud smile.

Damn. I'm surprised I came up with that.

"They need to ask us out first," Kyrn agreed.

"Good luck telling the guys that. 'Oh yeah by the way, Kyrn and Sam said you guys have to ask them out, because until then they aren't yours; even though you guys are mates'." She laughed.

"Well sorry if I want an actual relationship, and not one that assumes we are together," I said crossing my arms.

"I know I know. We should head back before the guys start freaking out. Who knows if they are done with their periods yet," she laughed standing up. "I swear they are on their periods every day from the way they act."

"I couldn't agree more," Kyrn agreed laughing.

"We should probably get back," Chloe suggested.

"Why?" I asked. We hadn't been out that long.

Chloe sighed and showed me her phone. "Zander is blowing up my phone asking when we are getting back."

"Damn," I sniggered as I handed her phone back and made my way for the door.

"The guys are freaking out."

"Shocker." Kyrn laughed as we piled in the car and made our way back to the house.

"There you girls are! What took you so long?" Jay growled out running outside.

"Told you." Chloe smirked at us.

"I'm confused," Xavier said, jogging up to me and wrapping me in his arms.

"Girl talk," I said while Kyrn and Chloe giggled.

The guys looked horrified.

"Don't want to know!" they yelled and ran back inside.

We shook our heads and followed them in.

"Hey, babe," Zander winked, walking up to Chloe and giving her a kiss.

"Oh my gosh! My poor innocent eyes!" I screamed, throwing my hands over my eyes.

"They won't be so innocent when I'm done mating with her." *What did Xavier just say? I hope he didn't just say that.*

I took my hands away and, sure enough, Xavier had said that; Jay was nodding and laughing.

I looked over at Chloe and Kyrn and they both had horrific looks on their faces. I'm guessing they heard that too.

"Excuse me?" I asked putting my hands on my hips and giving the death glare to Xavier.

His face paled and his eyes went wide.

"I-uh. I-I didn't say th-that," he stuttered.

The guys were on the floor laughing that Xavier had got caught.

"Uh huh. Then what *did* you say?" I pushed.

"You look really nice babe. You look absolutely gorgeous in that shirt." He tried to save himself.

And did it work? Nope! Not. At. All.

"Yea, that save didn't work," I said matter-of-factly.

"I know how much you love mint chocolate-chip ice cream. Jay and I will be right back. Come on Jay!" he called, dragging Jay outside by the hand into the car.

Once he shut the door I turned to see Chloe standing there, looking shocked.

"I can't believe he just said that. Well, whispered that, thinking I didn't hear him. But still!" I said laughing.

"Why did he get so perverted like all of the sudden? Oh wait, he got a mate. Stupid horny male wolves," Chloe replied shaking her hand.

"Yeah but you love it when I'm like that in bed," Zander said wiggling his eyebrows at Chloe.

She gasped and slapped his cheek slightly.

"Chloe! You dirty, dirty girl," Kyrn said shaking her head while 'tsking' her.

"But… That's not fair," she screamed. "Zander!"

His eyes went wide and he hauled ass upstairs with a very angry and red face, Chloe chasing after him.

"Why are all werewolves so perverted and dirty?" Kyrn asked me.

"Yeah. I'm starting to ask myself that question right now," I replied laughing. *This will be a very interesting relationship.*

When the boys made it back to the house, I pulled Xavier downstairs to talk.

"Okay. So I have some questions," I said sitting at the table drinking my water.

"Okay. Shoot," Xavier said leaning over it looking at me.

"So, what does it mean when your eyes glow?"

He laughed. "That means my wolf is there, but I'm still in control."

"What do you mean?"

"Well, um... Like. if I get too mad, my wolf wants to come out and show who is alpha. But even though he is there, I'm still in control. So every time my eyes are glowing, that's him," Xavier explained.

"Okay, another one. Earlier, your voice was really deep, and it held so much power. What was that about?"

"Okay, that time my wolf was in control."

"Your wolf is scary." I laughed.

He nodded in understanding. "I know. He's alpha and he has to let everyone know."

"Oh," I said. "He's still scary."

He stuck his tongue out at me chuckling. "Anything else, princess?"

"Uh, okay so earlier. Chloe said something about how I'm yours?"

He smiled and nodded again. "That's because you are."

"How?" I asked him completely confused.

He laughed. "You're my mate. So that means you are mine."

"That makes no sense."

He sighed. "It's a werewolf thing. Every werewolf has a mate. A mate is your soul mate. He or she is your everything. Once you find your mate, he or she is yours, and you belong to your mate. So that means I'm yours, and you're mine."

"But I'm not yours," I said in a d'uh tone.

Now it was his time to be confused. "What do you mean?" Xavier asked as his eyebrows furrowed together.

"I mean. I don't belong to you, so I'm not yours."

He growled and his eyes started to get that stormy gray color—he was mad. "You're my mate Sam. So you do belong to me, and you are mine."

"Technically, not really," I said smirking.

"How?" he asked getting mad.

I gave him an innocent smile. "You've never asked me out and I'm not your girlfriend. So therefore, I'm not yours."

With that I got up and left smiling in victory. That's how it's done.

***

Kyrn

"So how did he take it?" I asked Sam.

"He got mad for a second, but I think he finally understood that I'm not his until he asks me out," Sam said.

I laughed. "Yeah, Jay was the same way. He started growling, and I think I saw his eyes glow."

"Xavier was telling me about that stuff. I asked him some questions," Sam said.

"Same here. But, it's weird because I think I'm actually falling for Jay. Like, I can't really explain it. It's just, he's so funny, and nice, and hot. But he really is nice. He's so sweet and caring and hot and—"

"Oh my gosh!" Sam yelled cutting me off. "My poor ears." She laughed holding her hands over her ears.

"What?" I asked her.

"Gross!" She laughed. "Gosh, just go out with the guy."

"Nope. He's the guy, so he asks me out. Not the other way around."

"Touché," she said smiling.

"So did you tell him about the guy that was flirting with you?"

"Nope. And he will not find out. Got it?" Sam asked, threatening.

Over her shoulder I saw Xavier and Jay walking out of the kitchen. She's going hate me for this, but I think this will be entertaining. I smirked and she gave me a weird look. "Sure, Xavier will never know."

Xavier's head shot up at the sound of his name. "What will I not find out?" he asked walking to us.

Sam's eyes went wide.

Let me tell you, it was so hard to stop myself from laughing. My body started shaking and I had to cough a couple of times.

"Nothing," she said quickly.

Xavier turned toward me with an eyebrow raised. "Kyrn?"

I opened my mouth but Sam interrupted me yet again. "Don't. You. Dare," Sam said with narrowed eyes as I smiled.

I walked over to Jay and stepped behind him.

"A guy was flirting with Sam when we were with Chloe, and almost asked her on a date!" I blurted out.

"You traitor!" Sam yelled at me.

"He what?" Xavier yelled.

"Hey, Xavier. How have you been? Have you been working out or something?" Sam asked trying to get him to forget it.

"You have ten seconds to go run and hide princess," he said crossing his arms with a serious expression, but his lips were twitching up into a smile.

"Kyrn was only joking," she started, trying to save herself.

"Nine." He took a step closer to her.

"But—"

"Eight."

"Uh. Bye!" she yelled before running off.

"I need to go find her." He laughed.

"Don't you have to wait?" I asked.

"Hey. Chloe already told me. She flirted back." He smirked before running after her.

"I will never understand men," I told Jay.

"Now you know how we feel about women," he teased.

My mouth fell open and I slapped him across the face. Not hard at all. Not like it would really affect him at all anyway.

"What was that for?" he asked holding his cheek.

"Multiple things. A, kidnapping me. B, saying I'm yours when I'm not. And C, for making fun of the women's race," I said with a proud smile and walked into the living room.

And that was how we women did it.

Chapter 13: Boys Meet The Boys

Sam

I woke up to the feeling of something holding my waist.

I stiffened slightly and followed the arm to see Xavier snoring slightly. I relaxed and giggled at him. He groaned in his sleep and pulled me closer and nuzzled the back of my head.

Have you guys ever gotten that feeling where you have the sudden urge to pee? Yeah, well I have it right now.

I slowly tried to lift his arm up and failed miserably. It was like a freaking rock glued into place. It wouldn't budge. I groaned and tried to wiggle out.

"No," Xavier growled.

I froze thinking it was directed toward me, but I realized he was still sleeping.

Awe, he talks in his sleep. I'm going to have to bug him about that later.

I tried again and almost got out but both of his hands shot out and pulled me on top of him and he put his arms around my waist.

Could this get any worse?

I probably shouldn't have said that because the next thing I know, I'm now under Xavier. And he's still sleeping away and snoring.

"Mine." He smiled and put his face in the crook of my neck.

Does he always talk in his sleep?

"Xavier?" I asked trying to get my arms free.

He mumbled something but I couldn't understand it.

I managed to get one arm free and tried poking his cheek, but his cheek was too far away.

Time for plan B. I poked his side and his eyes shot open with a loud yelp. He fell off me onto the floor.

I can breathe!

Werewolves weigh a ton. But I'm not going to tell him that.

"What was that?" he asked looking around. I paused for a second before busting out laughing. "What?"

"Wh-who knew the big bad al-alpha was tick-ticklish," I strained to get out because I was laughing so hard.

He huffed and crossed his arms.

"So. There's nothing wrong with being ticklish," he defended while getting up and trying to reach me.

"No. I need to use the bathroom," I said before hopping off the bed and walking to the restroom.

"Hurry back! I need my little mate with me," I heard him yell through the closed door.

"Whatever." I laughed.

After I did my business, I walked out to see Xavier sprawled across his bed hugging my pillow and snoring.

"Yeah, need my little mate my ass." I laughed, walking out of the room and downstairs.

"Morning Sam," Kyrn and Jay said eating their cereal.

"Hey Kyrn. Hey everybody."

Chloe and Zander looked up and said hi, while Ryan, Hunter, and Tim did a nod while trying to focusing on playing Black Ops.

Men and their video games. But I probably shouldn't say much because Brett and I used to play Call of Duty all the time.

I quickly shook that memory off and grabbed an apple.

"Did you know Xavier talks in his sleep?" I asked them.

"You have no idea," Jay said while putting his bowl in the sink.

"He's also ticklish," I said with a smirk.

"Didn't know that one." Jay laughed with an evil glint in his eye.

"Yeah. He freaking rolled on top of me this morning. I went to go poke his cheek but I couldn't reach it, so I poked his side and he yelped and fell off the bed," I explained laughing.

"So that's what that loud thud was." Zander smiled.

"And let me tell you. He weighs a ton."

"I didn't think I was that fat," Xavier's voice filled the kitchen and I turned around seeing him poke his stomach. "But I could be wrong, because muscle weighs more than fat." He smirked while puffing out his chest and flexing his arms.

Yep, and there goes my mind thinking dirty thoughts again. Bad mind, bad mind.

"Sam?" A hand was waving in front of my face and the hand belonged to a smug looking Xavier.

That jerk.

"Yeah?" I asked.

"Did you see something you like?"

"No. Not really." I shrugged.

"Bu-u-u-urn," the guys said.

Xavier growled and stalked toward me.

"You sure?" He asked stepping right in front of me.

"Yeah. Now if it was Niall Horan or Dylan O'Brien, then that would be a different story. I mean those two, sexy!" I said with a sly smile.

"Oh my gosh, I know. Zayn. So hot," Chloe said, smiling.

"Don't forget Liam, guys," Kyrn joined in our little fan girl moment.

"Let's face it. They are all sexy. Along with the Teen Wolf guys. Yum," I said sighing.

Someone cleared their throat and I turned to see a pissed looking Xavier, along with a pissed looking Zander and Jay.

"Why have a teen wolf guy when you have your own Alpha wolf mate right here. And no more calling other men sexy except for me!" he growled and picked me up.

'Not this again.' I thought to myself with a sigh. "Fine. You ruin all the fun," I huffed.

He set me back down and nodded.

"Good." He gave me a peck on the cheek and headed for the fridge.

"Since we have the day off, what should we do?" Jay asked wrapping his arms around Kyrn. And man, was she blushing.

"I don't know. What do you guys think?" Xavier asked wrapping his arm around my hip.

Now I was the one blushing. Oh joy.

"Well, it's almost noon. We could all go out to eat?" Zander asked.

"Sounds good to me. Where do you ladies want to eat?"

"Awe, someone's being a gentleman." I laughed.

He smiled and nodded.

"Well, I'm kind of in the mood for pizza," Kyrn said looking at all of us.

"Oh. There's a Pizza Hut in town," Chloe said.

"Sounds good to me," I said agreeing.

"Well then, let's go," Kyrn said smiling and skipping to the door.

Pizza Hut, here we come!

So here we are in town, and Xavier thought it would be a good idea to park next to this really creepy alley, and Chloe, Kyrn, and I are all freaking out.

"You just had to park next to the creepy alley," I dragged out while getting out of the car.

"Don't worry princess, I'll protect you," Xavier teased while grabbing my hand.

I stuck my tongue out at him and continued walking.

As we were walking, I noticed a very familiar black Chevy truck in one of the parking spots next to the door. The truck turned off, suggesting people were about to get out.

I nudged Kyrn's arm and she looked over at me. I nodded my head toward the car, we both looked over. And guess who decided to get out. Brett and Trey.

I *knew* that truck looked familiar; it was Brett's truck. Brett and Trey saw us and gave us their famous smirks.

I looked at Kyrn and gulped.

Oh shit, I mouthed to her.

She groaned and nodded.

We walked inside and the waitress looked between Zander, Ryan, Xavier, and Jay with lust-filled eyes.

Umm, excuse me? Does she not see me holding his hand? I know we aren't dating, but still. I feel jealous.

Chloe cleared her throat and the chick snapped out of it and gave Chloe a death glare.

"Yeah, we need a table for seven. Thank you," she spat.

Too bad Hunter and Tim weren't here; they would have loved the attention. They had to go leave for a family dinner.

The girl, whose badge read 'Brittany', rolled her eyes and nodded.

Chloe, Kyrn, and I glared at her as we walked. When I sat down, I accidentally bumped her shoulder.

"Oops. Sorry." I smiled innocently at her.

Kyrn and Chloe snickered while the guys just looked confused.

"What would you guys like to drink?" Brittany asked Xavier.

"Um, I'll take a coke, two Sprites, lemonade, Mountain Dew, and two Pepsis. Thanks," Xavier said.

"Anytime." She winked and left to go get them.

I balled my fists up and closed my eyes trying to get my breathing under control.

Why am I getting so jealous? I've never been this jealous. It must be this mate thing.

She came back and handed us our drinks. She set the straws down. Well, she threw mine.

"Bitch," I mumbled.

"Excuse me?" she asked me putting her hands on her hips.

"Nothing. Oh my gosh, I love how you did you hair," I said faking excitement.

She rolled her eyes and asked us what we would like in our pizza.

After we ordered Xavier and Jay got up and just left.

"Uh, where are they going?" Kyrn asked.

Zander and Ryan shrugged while smiling.

"Do you guys know something?" I asked.

They looked at each other and slowly put their straws in their mouths.

"Um okay," I said. laughing.

We were having a good time until a waiter showed Brett and Trey to their table which was a couple away from us. Kyrn and I stiffened, but thankfully no one noticed.

Can we just have a break?

"Hey. We are back," Jay said, sitting down.

"Thanks for the warning," Chloe said.

"Thanks for the warning," Jay mocked back.

About twenty minutes later, the pizza had finally arrived.

And of course, Brittany. Joy. Kyrn and Chloe had the same annoyed facial expressions I did. I'm glad I'm not the only one.

"Here you are." She smiled, setting down the pizzas. "Let me know if you need anything," she batted her eye lashes to the guys and then finally left.

"'Bout time," Chloe said.

She reached for a piece of cheese, but she stopped and had a huge smile on her face.

I looked down and my eyes widened. When I saw the pizza, I started smiling like crazy.

Why, you might ask. Well on the pizza. written in white cheese. were the words, 'Sam, will you be my girlfriend?'.

"Will you?" Xavier asked hopefully.

"Yes." I nodded and hugged him.

He pulled back from the hug and leaned in a little. My breath hitched and he sighed and turned his head. *Oh come on Sam! Forget about what Brett did to you and kiss your new boyfriend.*

I grabbed his face and kissed him. On the lips. And boy what it amazing.

He was shocked for a second and returned the kiss by grabbing my hips.

"Hey. Save it for the bedroom." Chloe laughed.

We pulled apart and when I saw Xavier, he looked like a little kid in a candy store.

Which caused a blush to creep up on my cheeks.

"You look cute when you blush," he told me pulling me closer to him. "And guess what?"

"What?" I asked him.

"You are now officially mine. Well, you were mine when I first laid my eyes on you, but still... Now I'm the only one you can call sexy and flirt with," he said, pecking my lips.

I giggled and nodded.

"But Niall Horan and Dylan O'Brien are still sexy guys," I defended.

He growled a warning at me. "Sam."

"Just kidding." I laughed.

"Yes, we heard." I turned to see Kyrn kiss Jay.

'Bout time!

"There. Now you girls are ours," Jay said. We smiled and nodded as we started to eat.

When we finished our food and decided it was a good time to leave, the boys left a tip and paid.

"What did you think of that?" Kyrn asked Xavier as she held hands with Jay.

"I know how much Sam likes pizza." Xavier laughed as he smiled down at me. "I thought it would be a funny and cool idea."

Aw. I felt special.

"Yeah, she always did love pizza," a voice said behind us.

We turned around and Brett and Trey were standing there.

"Oh. You guys again," Chloe said with disgust.

"Oh, calm down," Brett said. Zander stood in front of Chloe and his eyes were getting black.

I looked at Trey and saw he had a face brace on.

99

I chuckled out loud, knowing that was because I'd punched him in the jaw.

"You okay, Sam?" Ryan asked me.

"I like your brace, Trey," I said calming down.

"Wait a minute. You're Trey?" Xavier asked.

Trey nodded and glared at me.

"So that means you're Brett," he pointed to Brett standing there. "Good to know," Xavier said, walking up to him and punched him right in the nose.

"Oh my gosh!" I yelled running up to them. "Xavier!"

He turned around and picked me up. "That's Brett. Your ex, right?"

"Yeah. But you don't have to punch him," I defended.

"I had a right to," he stated walking to the group.

I groaned and walked around him, and when I did, I felt a sharp pain in my right cheek.

"You freaking little— Brett yelled, but stopped when he saw it was me. "Sam! I-I didn't mean to…"

I cried out and fell to the ground from the impact, holding my cheek.

"Sam!" Xavier cried, crouching down next to me. He gently took hold of my cheek and I cried out again in pain.

He slowly stood up and turned to Brett's frightened looking face.

"You little bastard," Xavier growled as he clenched his fists.

Xavier lunged for Brett and tackled him to the ground.

"Chloe and Kyrn, take Sam to the car quickly," Jay said before he, Zander, and Ryan ran toward Xavier.

"Come on Sam," Chloe yelled over the noise.

She and Kyrn picked me up and walked me to the car.

"My face freaking hurts," I whispered letting tears come.

"I know babe," Kyrn soothed looking at my cheek. "Yeah, there's definitely going to be a mark."

"We can have the pack doctor look at it when we get back home," Chloe stated.

I did my best nod, although I didn't know what a pack doctor was. As if reading my mind Kyrn looked at Chloe.

"What's a pack doctor?" Kyrn asked.

"A pack doctor is pretty much a regular doctor. But he or she is also a werewolf and they know how to handle cuts, and bites, and other stuff like that," Chloe said as she carefully looked at my cheek.

Just then the door opened and a glowing-eyed Xavier came in and scooped me into his arms.

The guys were panting and Ryan took off right away. I turned my head the best I could and saw Brett's body lying there with Trey trying to get him to stand up.

"Are you okay?" Xavier's voice was deep and I'm guessing his wolf was there. He smiled. "Yes, it's Ryder speaking."

"I'm fine. But it hurts to talk," I replied quietly.

He growled and put his face in my neck and stiffed. "I'm sorry."

"Okay. I've been meaning to ask you this. Why do you sniff me?" I asked as I pulled back to look at him.

He chuckled and closed his eyes. When he opened them again, they were back to their normal gray color.

"It helps calm my wolf down when he is upset or worrying if you're safe or not," Xavier mumbled as he eyed my cheek.

"Oh," I said.

"Let's go get your cheek checked out shall we?"

I nodded and laid my good cheek on his shoulder while he wrapped his arm around me.

Today had been lovely.

Chapter 14: The Fight

Xavier

That shit deserved to be punched.

"Oh my gosh!" Sam yelled running up to me. "Xavier!"

I turned around and picked her up, sniffing her neck. I could feel my wolf purring in my mind. Horny wolf.

"That's Brett. Your ex, right?" I asked as I looked at him lying on the ground.

"Yeah. But you don't have to punch him!" Sam yelled.

Why is she protecting him? I walked over and set her down on the ground.

"I had the right to," I said, pissed. She groaned and walked around me, probably to check on him. Wait, I don't want her going anywhere near him!

"You little... Sam! I-I didn't mean to," Brett yelled.

I heard a loud smack and someone cry out in pain. I whipped around and saw Sam on the ground holding her cheek.

"Sam!" I yelled running over to her and crouching down.

I gently took hold of her face and slowly removed her hand. Her cheek had a fist print on it, and it was quickly turning purple and blue. Her cheek was getting huge.

"You little bastard!" I yelled turning toward a shaking Brett. I lunged for him and barely heard what Jay said to the girls. I threw a punch to his face and he fell backwards on the concrete.

"St-stop. I didn't mean t-to," he said trying to block my punches.

"You punched Sam!" I yelled threw my punches.

"Xavier! Stop! You're going to kill him," Zander yelled grabbing my arm.

And that's a bad thing? Why?

"Hey! Stop punching him," Trey yelled.

I stopped immediately and gave him a glare.

"You better shut up or you're going to get punched too," I threatened.

He put his hands up and slowly backed up. Smart kid. Jay came and stopped in front of me and put his hands on my shoulder.

"You need to stop before you kill him," he stated calmly.

It was hard to calm down. I'd just watched my mate get punched in the face by her ex-boyfriend. I couldn't calm down. I felt my wolf coming up, and I'm pretty sure my eyes shifted to glowing gray color. My wolf was close to getting out and ripping this kid up into shreds.

"It's hard," I said.

"I know. You need to focus. I'm upset just like you are. He punched our Luna. But we can't have you shifting and killing a human. Especially the ex-boyfriend of your mate," he pointed out.

I sighed. He was right. Even though he'd been a complete ass to her, she wouldn't forgive me if I killed him.

"Fine," I growled. Jay and Zander nodded and took their hands off me.

Okay, maybe one last punch will do. But, the poor guy just got off the ground. Oh well. I smirked and punched him one more time right in the nose.

"Here's some advice, don't go near Sam or Kyrn." I glared at him. He gave me a weak nod. "That goes for you too." I pointed to Trey.

He glared but nodded.

I smiled and began to walk away. I felt my wolf push through finally, and he had us running toward the car. He pulled Sam onto his lap and they started talking.

Ryan took off right away and I think we were heading back home. I heard someone say 'pack doctor', but I was kind of zoned out at the moment. I wasn't really paying attention that much. I was mainly focused on my mate and making sure she was okay.

The next thing I know is, we are parked in front of the house of the pack's doctor.

***

Sam

"So. Who is this guy?" I whispered to Chloe.

We have finally arrived at the pack doctor and he was tall, like really tall.

He had chocolate brown hair, with a pair of chocolate brown eyes to match. He had a bright smile, he was skinny, but he had muscle on his arms, and he was tall. But you already knew that.

"He's the pack doctor." She laughed.

I gave her an 'I-already-know-that look.'

She giggled and finally answered my question. "His name is Dr. Tom. He's a really good doctor, so don't worry."

I nodded, unsure, but I trusted Chloe.

We kept on walking, into this white room that looks exactly like a mini hospital. It's kind of creepy if you ask me.

"You can take a seat right there, Luna." The doc smiled.

Luna? Oh d'uh, that's right. I'm still not use to this stuff yet. He pointed to the chair thing and I nodded. I sat down, still holding my cheek.

"So what happened today?" Tom asked.

"She got punched," Xavier breathed out, balling his fists.

Tom's head snapped to mine and his eyes were growing darker and darker.

Xavier's eyes did that too.

I'm trying to remember what he said about that, oh yea. His wolf was mad. Wait, so why is Tom mad?

"Dr. Tom, it's okay," Chloe soothed. "Xavier got revenge. Big time."

Tom closed his eyes and breathed deeply. He reopened his eyes and wrote something down on his clipboard.

"What just happened?" I asked.

Ryan smiled. "His wolf got mad."

"Why?" I asked him.

"He's part of the pack Sam. His wolf just heard that his Luna got hurt. Members of the pack are very protective of their Luna and alpha. So when he and his wolf heard that, his wolf wasn't very happy," he explained.

"Oh. That kind of makes sense."

"Kind of?" He asked amused.

I laughed but stopped because it hurt my face.

"In my defense, I'm still trying to get used to this stuff. But, I'm starting to get some of it," I retorted.

"That's good," he said sitting down.

"Okay Luna. I'm going to need to run some x-rays but I'm going to need to look at your cheek first," Tom said carefully.

"No." I shook my head. I don't want him anywhere near my face let alone touching it. He gave me a warm smile.

"Luna, I need to look at it." Tom sighed.

I looked over at Xavier and he gave me a small nod.

I sighed and turned back to Tom. "Okay," I mumbled.

He'd better not hurt me. He smiled and gently took hold of my hand and removed it.

"Oh wow," he said.

He held onto my chin and ran a finger over my cheek bone.

I hissed in pain and smacked his hand away.

Xavier shot out of his seat and growled, "Careful!"

"I'm sorry alpha, but I had to touch it to see where we are at," Tom replied calmly.

Xavier growled again, but reluctantly sat back down.

"Okay. I'm pretty sure it's broken, but we will have to do an x-ray to be sure. So if you will please lie down, we can get started," Tom said quickly as he wrote something in his clipboard.

I lay down and he started with the x-rays. And let me tell you, it was painful. He had to keep moving my head everywhere; When he moved my head into this one position, it took everything in me to not cry out in pain.

Ten minutes later, we were finally done with the x-rays. It took some time to see what was actually wrong with it, but it turns out I have a crack in my cheek bone, my jaw is slightly shifted over, and my nose is a little crooked.

Tim gave me this weird plastic face mask thing for my cheek; it has a metal strap that's curved so it fits over my nose. It didn't touch my eyes and it stopped just under my nose. But he did have to get my jaw back into place. And that wasn't a very good feeling to feel.

I was holding onto Xavier's hand the entire time and I squeezed his hand so hard that even he winced.

"And we are finally done," Tom said tightening up the last strap to my mask. "There you are, Luna. You guys may go home now. But, I don't want you eating big pieces of food, since I'v had to shift your jaw back into place. Your jaw will be weak because of the movement and you will be in pain for quite some time. So, I will need you to take some pain medication for it. Two; one in the morning and two more before you go to bed."

"Okay." I winced from the pain, and Tom chuckled.

"Try to not talk so much also." He laughed. "Try getting a dry-erase board and you can talk that way. You can talk if you want, but it will be very painful."

I shook my head. I want the dry-erase board. I turned to Xavier and nodded.

"You want the dry-erase board?" he asked, smiling. I gave him a nod. "Okay. Zander and I will go get one for you."

I gave him a hug for a thank you and he hugged me back.

"Anytime princess," he said as he kissed my forehead.

The doctor gave me my medicine and some more rules, like showering and sleeping. This is going to be fun.

Can you detect my sarcasm?

Chapter 15: No Talking

Sam

I hadn't talked at all and I was just now realizing how hard it actually is.

We finally got back from the doctor and Xavier and Zander left to go get me a dry-erase board. I hoped he'd get me a colored marker. I didn't want black. That was too plain. I wanted some fun colors. Oh! Maybe he'd get me purple. Or blue. Or green.

A couple of minutes later, Xavier and Zander walked through the door. I ran up to him and smiled.

"Hey babe," he said opening his arms up. I grabbed the bag and turned around and sat at the table, getting out the board. I turned around and winked at Xavier. "Wow. Thanks Sam. I'm really feeling the love."

I smiled and got the marker out and held the board. He got me a green marker. Yay!

I wrote on the board for him. *You're welcome.*

"Ha ha. Aren't you just really funny today," he teased. I flashed him a sweet smile and he scoffed. "Where's my hug and kiss?"

I don't know. I wrote.

He growled playfully and ran toward me.

I wasn't paying attention because I was erasing my board, when I felt his arms go around my waist. I jumped in surprise and Xavier placed a kiss on my neck. It took everything in my will power to not let out a moan.

"Princess, can I have my hug and kiss?" he asked blowing air on my neck.

I'm so glad I can't talk; it would have sounded like a mess of words. I nodded and turned around. He placed a soft kiss on my lips, being careful of my jaw.

"Thanks, princess." He got up and walked into the living room.

Well then, Xavier.

I felt lonely so I got up and went in there and sat on the couch.

"Hey Sam. How are you feeling?" Ryan asked me.

Okay I guess, I wrote.

He laughed and I gave him a questionable look.

"You have to write everything down." He smirked.

I glared at him and he put his hands up in surrender.

I might be in pain, but I can still punch you, I wrote back with my own smirk.

He let out a nervous laugh. "You wouldn't hurt me. Right?"

I shrugged and got up to get a movie.

"Oh, she would." I turned around to see Kyrn and Jay walking over to the other couch. "I mean, she did punch Trey."

"This is true," he agreed.

"My little princess is a badass," Xavier said with a proud smile. "Speaking of which Jay, we need to get the girls into training soon."

"What?" Kyrn asked.

"Since you guys are human and aren't as strong as us." He paused and I rolled my eyes. "You guys need to learn how to protect yourselves if any of us can't protect you. You are the Luna and beta female of this pack, so it makes complete sense," Xavier said, sitting up.

I groaned and Kyrn spoke up. "But... We pretty much did kick Hunter's, Tim's, and Ryan's asses that day."

"I know, but still... I need to have you guys train. And that's final."

I glared at him and he smirked at me. *Jerk,* I wrote on the board.

"Sorry princess. But we have to do it. I can't lose you," Xavier admitted, as he pulled me closer to him.

I huffed and nodded.

Training? Yeah, I don't really want to do that. I'll pass thank you very much.

"What movies do you guys want to watch?" Kyrn asked sitting next to me and going through the movies.

I looked through the pile and saw The Conjuring.

I smiled and held it up.

"That one?" Chloe asked unsure.

I nodded and put it in.

"I'm going to die!" Kyrn shouted as she ran over to Jay and snuggled up into his side.

There's an 'A-awe' moment.

I smiled and ran to the kitchen to go get some snacks.

"Need some help?" Chloe and Zander asked me.

I nodded gratefully at them and they chuckled. We grabbed all the snacks and drinks and headed back into the living room. We got everything settled and took our seats in the chairs and couches, with Ryan on the floor.

Ryan needs to find a mate.

"Ready?" Xavier asked us.

Once we all nodded, he pressed play and the movie started.

Have you guys ever got that moment where you realized that whatever you did was a bad idea? Yeah, well, maybe watching this movie was a bad idea. This movie is creepy as hell!

My side is pressed up against Xavier's chest and his arms are wrapped tightly around me. I have a blanket in front of my face and Xavier keeps on laughing at me. Kyrn is pretty much sitting on Jay, literally. And Chloe, well she is pretty much hiding behind Zander. And Ryan? He was hiding his face with a pillow.

"It's just a movie, princess," Xavier said in my ear.

"Still," I whispered trying not to move my jaw.

He held me tighter and kissed my temple. "I'm right here."

I nodded and focused on the movie again.

I jumped at the part where the lady was at the stairs or whatever, and the hands came out of the shadows and clapped.

Kyrn screamed, which then in turn caused Chloe to scream and she threw the popcorn across the room landing directly on Ryan. Poor guy.

The movie finally ended. Kyrn looked like she was about to cry, Chloe was just staring at the TV, and I was too scared to move.

"I think they're scared," Zander joked.

Chloe snapped out of it and chucked a pillow at his head.

"Ow!" he groaned as he rubbed his head.

"Whoops." She smiled and got up from the couch and walked up the stairs.

"Women," he said before following her.

"How do you think men would be if there weren't any girls on this earth?" Jay asked.

"Not as horny," Kyrn said.

Jay glared at her and she smiled before heading up the stairs.

"I agree with Zander," he said before following her up.

"Ready to go to bed, princess?" Xavier asked.

"Yes I am." Ryan laughed giving him a hug. "Will you carry me?"

"No," Xavier teased.

Ryan pouted.

"Well then. I'm going to bed. It's like midnight." Ryan left and it was just me and Xavier.

Xavier came to me and picked me up. I hate it when he does this. Well, at least he's not throwing me over his shoulder like he always did before. That actually hurt quite a few times and I did have a bruise on my stomach, but I'd never told him.

I glared at him the entire way up the stairs. He didn't pay me any attention, but by the cute little smirk plastered on his face, he knew I was annoyed.

We got to our room and he gently set me down on the bed while he got dressed for bed.

I was blushing furiously when he took his shirt and pants off, leaving him only in his boxers. *This just isn't fair.*

"You look cute when you blush," he said crawling into bed. I stuck my tongue out at him and rolled over. "Goodnight, babe."

I smiled and turned back over so I could cuddle into his chest. I gave him a soft peck on the lips and rested my head on his shoulder. He tightened his arms around me and pulled me closer.

I closed my eyes and fell into a nice, peaceful sleep.

Chapter 16: Beaten By A Human

Sam

It'd been a month since my broken jaw and I didn't have to wear that stupid, repulsive, ugly mask anymore. As you can tell, I hated that piece of plastic. And I can talk normally.

But the doctor still said I shouldn't do any hard core physical activity for a couple weeks, and that means I'm out of training!

Ha ha, suck on that Kyrn!

She still has to do it, and Xavier was making me go to all of her training sessions so I will have an idea of what I'd do when I was fully healed.

And since Jay is the beta, he is the training instructor for the whole pack.

Zander is the assistant, so whenever Jay isn't there, Zander takes over. Hunter and Tim help out with training as well since they are the top warrior wolves. Or guard wolves, or whatever they were called. All I knew was, they were really powerful and strong.

So here I am, sitting in a chair talking to Hunter and Tim while Zander is teaching Kyrn some moves.

Xavier and Jay had to go to a meeting of some sort and since it's five in the morning, Chloe is still sleeping. Lucky little brat.

I stopped thinking and my eyes started to become heavy.

"Sam?" I heard a voice next to me. I groaned and tried to hit his face. "Sam. Stop hitting me." The voice laughed.

"Go away. I'm too tired," I mumbled.

"No. Alpha Xavier said you have to watch Kyrn and Zander train so you know what you are going to have to do," he spoke softly.

I slowly opened my eyes, but not all the way, and looked to see Hunter with a small smile on his face.

"No," I mumbled and turned my head.

"Yes Sam. Sorry, but alpha Xavier sai-" I interrupted him by poking his nose, then his cheek, and then his forehead. "What are you doing?" he asked, laughing.

"Trying to find the off button," I said poking around his face some more.

He laughed and grabbed my hand. "Watch."

I stuck out my tongue at him and turned in my seat to see Zander pinning Kyrn down on the ground.

"Always pay attention to your opponent. And always expect the unexpected," I heard Zander say to a very annoyed Kyrn.

He jumped up and turned around to dust off his clothes.

Kyrn grabbed a rock and started twirling it around in her hands as she stood up.

"Now. Remember Kyrn, you always have to—Ow!" Zander screamed rubbing his forehead.

Yeah, that rock that Kyrn had? Well, she kind of threw it at Zander's head.

"Ugh. This is completely pointless!" she screamed at him.

He sighed and pinched the bridge of his nose. "Kyrn. Calm down-"

"Easy for you to say! You're a freaking wolf. You have super strength. I'm taking a break," she said breathing in deeply.

"Kyrn. You know we can't do that."

"Watch me," she scowled and stormed toward the house. When she got there, she opened the door and slammed it shut.

I dragged a hand down my face. "I'll go talk to her."

I got up and followed her path to the house. When I walked in, the living room and the kitchen were empty.

"Kyrn?" I called out.

"Upstairs," she called back.

I walked up the stairs to hers and Jay's room to find her lying down in the bed with her face in the pillows.

"You okay?" I asked her.

"No! Does he honestly expect me to take him down? He's a freaking wolf, Sam. A wolf! I can't pin a wolf down to the ground," Kyrn said as she threw her pillow across the room.

"We did to Tim, Ryan, and Hunter no problem," I told her remembering back to that day.

That was a fun day now that I think about it.

"Zander is stronger than all three of them. You know that," Kyrn pointed out.

"True. But just try to focus on him now. Let your energy run throughout your body Kyrn. Focus on it."

"Maybe you should be the teacher," she joked.

"I wish. I could probably do a better job than Mr. Grumpy-pants out on the field." I laughed.

She chuckled along with me and stood up.

"Thanks, Sam," Kyrn smiled.

"Of course, Kyrn. That's what sisters are for."

"Forever together," she said pulling me into a hug.

"Now come on. Let's go see you kick some wolf-ass." I winked.

She nodded and we walked downstairs.

As we passed the basement, I got a great idea. I stopped and pulled Kyrn to a stop as well.

"What?" she asked me.

"I have an idea." I smirked.

"Oh great. You and your great ideas. Just fantastic. They always seem to get us in trouble," Kyrn said rolling her eyes. "What is it this time?"

"Well," I paused and looked at the door. "They never said anything about not using martial art weapons."

She smirked at me. "Keep talking."

"You know how Zander said 'Always pay attention to your opponent. And always expect the unexpected'?"

"Yeah?" Kyrn agreed confused.

"Well, let's make his eat his own words."

"But, Sam," Kyrn said as her eyebrows furrowed.

"Kyrn. Just do it. They're men. They don't think we are smart or good enough. Go show him who's boss," I told her.

"How am I supposed to do that when he can flip me over and pin me down in a matter is seconds?"

"The daggers," I said remembering the fight we had with Hunter, Tim, and Ryan.

"What are you doing?" she asked me as I grabbed a pair of daggers.

"Use his words against him. But don't use them right away. Give him the illusion that you are just simply dodging his attacks," I told her, handing her the daggers.

She gave me a smirk and nodded. "Got it."

We made our way toward the door and opened it.

We walked back outside to see a very pissed of Zander.

"Where the hell have you been? We are supposed to be training," Zander growled.

"Calm down wolfie. I'm ready," Kyrn said walking right past him to the field.

"Don't call me that," he growled and followed her.

I sat back on my seat, with Hunter and Tim walking over to me to sit down as well.

"What did you say to her to make her all pumped up?" Tim asked.

I gave him a sly smile. "You'll see."

"Dude. I know that smile. Something's going to happen. And it's never good. Good things never happen when Sam has that smile on."

"Well, let's see what happens," Hunter said looking over at Kyrn and Zander.

"Ready?" Zander asked.

"Ready," Kyrn confirmed.

She started dodging like she always did at the martial arts class.

"Why is she dodging like that?" Tim asked.

115

"Look at her. She's on fire!" Hunter said amazed.

"She has her own fighting style. Remember when we kicked your guys' asses that day?" I asked.

"Yeah, what about it?"

"Remember how she dodged you guys when you tried to grab her."

"Yeah."

"Well, when we took our martial arts classes, with each weapon is a different fighting style. And a different fighting style also comes with a different defense style. She's pretending Zander has daggers, and that's how she's dodging him so easily now. She's focusing on him and not her surroundings. So, she's using her fighting style," I explained to them.

I smiled in victory as Zander kept missing Kyrn.

"Oh. That's awesome," Tim exclaimed.

"So, by pretending he has daggers, she's doing a better job?" Hunter asked.

I nodded. "By pretending he has daggers her mind is telling her she is fighting someone who has daggers, so her body is reacting like it did during the classes."

He nodded in understanding and was about to say something, but we heard Zander talking instead.

"Nice moves, Kyrn. What made you get your head in the game?" Zander asked as Kyrn dodged a punch.

"Sam." Was all she said before she lunged at his legs and took him to the ground.

He yelped in surprise and Kyrn reached under her shirt and pulled the daggers out.

She stuck them through his shirt so he was stuck to the ground. Then she pulled out another dagger from the strap around her ankle and put it at his throat.

"What the hell!" he yelled. "This isn't training with daggers, Kyrn. We are supposed to use our fists."

116

"No. You never said that. You just called it training," Zander growled and didn't move so Kyrn continued talking. "Oh, and Zander?"

"What?" he asked through clenched teeth.

Kyrn gave him a victory smile. "Always pay attention to your opponent. And always expect the unexpected."

With that she got off him and walked over toward me.

I stood up clapping and met her half way.

"I'm really impressed," I said.

She did a little curtsey. "Why thank you."

We looked over and saw Zander still lying on the ground with the daggers through his shirt trapping him there. He had a shocked expression on his face from getting a taste of his own medicine.

"That was awesome Kyrn!" Tim said running up to us.

"Good thing I videotaped that," I said waving Hunter's phone in the air.

"Is that my phone?" Hunter asked patting his pockets.

I nodded and gave it back to him. "I wanted to use it so I could show Kyrn the goods and the bads. Hope you don't mind."

"Nah, it's cool. And besides, now we get to watch Zander get his ass kicked by a human," Hunter winked.

We busted out laughing at that.

"That is true. And I also got the part where Kyrn quoted the words Zander said earlier, and Zander's expression afterwards," Tim chuckled.

We all kept laughing after that and Zander walked over and dropped the daggers by our feet.

"Yeah, yeah. It's so hilarious," he growled out and walked back to the house.

We stood up, wiping away our tears, and headed inside. Today is going to be a good day.

Chapter 17: Biting The Human

Sam

After Kyrn's training we walked into the house to see Chloe stuffing food in her mouth and Zander laughing at her.

"Oh, this is gold," Hunter said.

She glared at him and swallowed her food. "How did training go?"

Zander groaned and slammed his head on the table.

"Zander got his ass kicked by a girl," I said teasing him.

"She used daggers. It wasn't fair," Zander retorted.

"You're the werewolf and third in command. I'm pretty sure that's fair babe," Chloe stated rubbing his back.

"You're supposed to be on my side," he whined.

"Oh, right, sorry. Um… Kyrn. That's not very fair to use martial arts weapons on the teacher," Chloe accused shaking her head at us. "How was that?"

"Better," Zander said before he kissed her cheek.

"Always expect the unexpected," Kyrn said with a smile walking over to the fridge.

"And we got the whole thing videotaped," I said high-fiving Hunter.

"What did you get videotaped?" a male voice asked.

I turned around to see Xavier and Jay walk in.

"Xavier!" I yelled running into him and pulling him into a giant hug.

"Oof," I heard him say before he wrapped his arms around my waist and put his face into my neck. "Did ya miss me?"

I nodded and looked at his face.

"And no more waking me up at five in the damn morning," I huffed and walked back to the chair.

He chuckled and sat next to me.

"How did training go Kyrn?" Jay asked walking over to her.

"I kicked his ass!" she replied smiling like crazy.

"And we got the whole thing videotaped," Tim said, handing them Hunter's phone.

They sat down and watched it. After it was down, their faces held shock before they erupted into laughter.

"That was priceless. Did you see his face?" Jay asked.

"I sure did. Here's your phone back," Xavier got out in between his laughs.

"Speaking of phones, can I have mine?" I asked.

Xavier stopped laughing and looked at me. "Um."

"Please. My parents are probably worried sick," I begged with the puppy dog face.

"If we get you two your phones, you won't run away or anything?"

I smacked him upside the head. "Do you think I would try to run away when I already accepted you?"

Xavier winced and rubbed the back of his head before looking down.

"No," he spoke quietly.

"Idiot," I said and grabbed a water bottle.

"Heard that."

"You were meant to."

"Fine. We can go tomorrow to go get your stuff," Xavier agreed.

"Thanks," I said giving him a peck on the lips.

"You're welcome, princess."

Did I ever mention how cute it was when he called me princess? If I didn't, well, it's really cute.

"So when does Sam get to train with me?" Kyrn asked curious.

"Kyrn! Shut up!" I yelled, laughing.

She winked at me and I groaned.

"We are going to another check up at the end of this week. And if the doctor says she can train, then she gets to," Xavier said wrapping his arm around my shoulders and pulling me into him.

"Not going," I defended.

"Yes, you are," he shot back.

"Why do I even have to go in the first place?"

"You're the Luna. If I can't protect you or any of our pack members can't, then you're going to need to protect yourself."

"I hate everything," I said slamming my head on the table.

"No. Bad Sam," Xavier said stopping my head from hitting the table again.

"I'm not a dog like you." I smiled innocently at him.

He glared at me playfully before smiling. He dipped his head down toward mine and licked my cheek.

"Ew!" I screamed and jumped up. "What the hell was that for?" I asked frantically wiping my face.

"You said I was a dog. And dogs show their affection by licking their companions, so I licked your cheek," Xavier said shrugging like it was no big deal.

"You're disgusting." I laughed. "No more licking me."

"No promises," he muttered. I shot him a look of disbelief and he chuckled nervously. "My wolf's fault."

"Sure, blame it on your poor innocent wolf," I

"Trust me. He's not so innocent. You should hear some of the stuff he thinks about."

"Like what?"

"He talks about what he wants to do to yo— I mean the food that he hunts," he covered up.

Was he really going to say that? That his wolf wants to do stuff to me. I'm a little scared to know. Does he want to, like, kill me or something? But whatever it is, I really don't want to know.

I let it slide, although I was a little curious about what he was going to say. I made a mental note to ask Chloe later. "Whatever." I shrugged and walked into the living room.

A minute later everyone joined me except for Hunter, Tim, and Ryan. They always ended up disappearing somewhere.

"Patrol," Xavier said. He must have seen the confused look on my face. I nodded and sat on the couch. Well, more like sprawled across the couch. I didn't feel like sharing. But did that stop Xavier? No-o-o. Of course not.

He decided he wanted to pick me up and place me on his lap and hold me like I was a little child. "Can I help you?" I asked him.

"Nope." He shook his head and moved mine so it was in his neck and held me tightly.

I don't know what's happening. I was a little confused as to why he was doing this, but it made my entire body relax and my mind just went blank. I soon molded my body more into his and closed my eyes. I heard him chuckle as he kissed my forehead. When I looked up at him he had a proud smile in his face. Why? I have no idea.

The guys started talking and I found myself falling asleep in his arms.

I woke up with a dry mouth. I looked over at the clock and saw that the time was 2:47 a.m. Wow, I must have really been tired. I untangled myself from Xavier's arms and he tried pulling me back. But I got up faster.

After I got my glass of water from the bathroom I walked back in the bedroom seeing Xavier looking frantically around the room. I giggled softly and turned on the light. "What are you doing?"

His head snapped up and I met his eyes. They were close to black, meaning his wolf was close to the surface. He ran toward me, lifting me up in his arms. "There you are."

"Dude. I was getting a drink."

"I didn't know that. All I know is that I reached over to pull you closer to me and I didn't feel your body there. Then I shot out of bed and my wolf was freaking out."

"Couldn't he feel me in the bathroom?" I asked.

"Well," he started but never finished.

"You were freaking out too much, were you?" I asked but I already knew the answer.

"Pft. No," he said pulling us over to the bed.

"Ri-i-ighht." I smiled at him.

He smiled back at me and pulled me in his lap. He put his face in my neck and lightly kissed it. Shit. It's hard holding in a moan. I bit my lip trying to stop it and succeeded.

He pulled his head back and gave me his famous smirk. "Why are you biting your lip?"

"Um," I said but I couldn't finish anything.

"You okay?" he asked, smiling. I nodded and he gave me a chuckle before capturing my lips with his.

When he kissed me, my worries, fears, everything melted away. I kissed back and a low possessive growl escaped his throat and he wrapped his arms tighter around me.

After a couple of minutes I pulled back and needed a breath. But that didn't stop him as he trailed kisses across my jaw line and down the side of my neck. A shiver ran through my body as he kissed a certain spot where my neck and shoulder meet. A loud moan came out and he smiled against my skin.

He sucked on that spot and my hand tightened on his shirt. "Xavier," I said softly.

"Yes?" he asked against my neck.

"Please," I begged. I wanted him to put his mark there to show the world I was his.

The first time I heard about the biting and the mating process, I thought it was weird and didn't like the idea of my werewolf mate biting my neck just to show everyone that I was taken. I thought it was stupid and unnecessary, but now, my body is craving it. Like I need to have the mark.

"Please what?" he asked. But I'm pretty sure he already knew what I was going to say.

"Please bite, or mark me, or whatever it's called," I rushed out.

"Is Sam asking me to mark her?" He teasingly asked. I nodded my head and sighed in content as he kissed the spot again. "That would involve biting your neck though."

"I don't care." That's all it took for him to kiss that spot one last time before I felt really sharp teeth make their way through my neck.

My scream turned into a moan and I relaxed further into his arms. I tilted my head over so he had more access to my neck.

After a few minutes he pulled back, and I felt him lick it. "Why did you do that?" I was surprised at how my voice sounded. It was raspy and my body felt amazing that it was hard to breathe, the pleasure was so breathtaking.

"I had to close it so it could heal. By the way, you taste delicious," his voice sounded just as breathless as mine. I smiled at him and pecked his lips.

"You won't eat me now right?" I teased.

"Oh course not. Just might do a lot of biting you," he wiggled his eyebrows.

"Perv."

"Kidding."

No you're not. Silly Xavier.

I yawned. "I'm tired."

"It's common. You are going to be tired after I bite you. Just lay your head down and we can go back to sleep." I nodded my head and allowed him to lay my head on his chest.

When my head made contact with his chest, I was out.

Chapter 18: Angry Moms

Sam

I stood in front of Kyrn with my mouth open, and hers was too.

"You," we both said.

After I woke up to find a note saying Xavier left to go to patrol with Jay and Zander, I walked downstairs to see Kyrn wearing a tank top and something on her neck.

"You got marked?" she asked me, smiling,

I nodded. "So, did you." She blushed and nodded as well. "Let me guess, after you guys went upstairs?"

"Yeah. You?"

"At like three in the morning." I laughed. "I was thirsty and after I got my drink, I came back into the room seeing Xavier frantically looking around the room."

"I would have loved to see that. Was he, like, running around or something?" Kyrn asked with a smirk.

"That. And looking in our closets and under the bed."

"Oh, wow."

"It was a sight to see." I giggled.

"Oh, finally the Luna and beta female are up," Hunter said in a teasing matter.

"Hunter," Kyrn whined. "You know you aren't supposed to call us that unless we are in a very important situation."

"My apologies, Luna and beta female." He bowed.

"Hunter," she warned.

"Yes, beta female?" He smirked.

She gave him a sweet smile and turned toward the fridge and opened it up. She reached inside and took out the chocolate syrup.

When he saw it, his eyes went wide.

"Dude, I'd run if I was you," I said laughing.

He turned toward me for a split second before sprinting out of the kitchen and out into the back yard.

Kyrn screamed and ran after him.

"What happened? I heard Kyrn scream!" Tim said running in the kitchen with glowing eyes.

I turned around and jumped when I saw his eyes.

"Calm down, Tim. She is chasing Hunter around the backyard," I said quickly so he wouldn't go into beast mode.

He visibly relaxed and his eyes went back to normal. "Oh. Wait. Why?"

"Long story short, Hunter was mocking her, she got out the chocolate syrup, and now she is chasing him around the backyard," I explained with a shrug.

"He will never learn. She always catches him."

"He might be one of the best warriors, but if he's playing, he doesn't have good balance." I laughed.

"I agree. When they come back inside and Hunter takes a shower, shall we gather up some more wolves and head to your house?"

"Sure. Sounds good to me." I nodded.

We kept talking about anything really, and then we heard the back door open.

Kyrn walked in first with a smug expression before she headed upstairs.

About a minute later, Hunter strolled in, covered with chocolate syrup from head to toe.

"Some advice. If you're running from Kyrn, get a head start." Hunter sighed.

Tim and I broke into fits of laughter and he pulled his phone out and took a picture of Hunter. Hunter flipped him off before he walked upstairs.

"Come on. Let's go get ready," Tim said.

I nodded and we went upstairs.

Finally everyone was ready and we made our way to the car.

The ride to my house didn't feel that long actually. Probably because we were having a dance party in the car and screaming to Brittany Spears. Yes. It was one of those moments.

We grabbed all of my stuff I needed and headed back to Xavier's house.

But have you ever got that feeling of being absolutely terrified when you didn't pick up your phone when your mom called you? Well, being absolutely terrified is a complete understatement.

After we got home our houses and picked up my phone and clothes, I had twenty missed calls and thirty-five texts from mom, ten missed calls and twenty-five texts from dad, and a couple from Kyrn's parents.

Here goes nothing. I picked up my phone and called my mom back.

Ring

Ring

"Samantha Lynn Conner! Where the hell have you been? Your father and I have tried calling you and you never once picked up the damn phone!" my mom screamed from the other end.

"Well. I...Uh." What am I supposed to say? I was kidnapped by my werewolf boyfriend/mate and so was Kyrn?

"Well?" she asked impatiently.

"Um. Mine and Kyrn's phones died. So when we took them to the phone store, the guy said our batteries were fried. So, we ordered new ones and they didn't come until today. And he never gave us phones to use until our batteries came in. That's why we didn't get hold of you guys. Sorry to worry you, mom," I lied.

I can't believe I came up with that. Damn, I give myself props.

"What about the home phone?" she asked in a matter-of-fact tone.

"You disconnected last month. Remember?" I laughed at her.

"Oh," she said, chuckling. "Right. Sorry for freaking out, dear."

"It's okay, Mom."

"Okay. Well I'll go tell your father and Kyrn's parents. Talk to you later, dear. Love you."

"Okay Mom. Love you too." With that I hung up and breathed a sigh of relief.

"Hey Sam. I should probably call my mom," Kyrn said walking into my room.

"Okay. Make sure when she's asks you why you haven't been answering, you say our phone batteries were fried and that our new batteries didn't come in until today. Oh! And that the phone guy didn't give us replacement phones. I already called my mom and told her."

"Okay thanks." Kyrn left the room and I lay down on my bed. I must have dozed off or something because I heard the door open.

"Sam baby. Wake up," a deep soothing voice said next to me.

"Hmm?" I mumbled and turned away from the voice.

"Come princess. Time to get up," I heard a chuckle and felt something poking my cheek. I swatted the hand away and groaned. "Don't make me do this," he threatened.

"Go away."

"Fine." There was a pause before he was poking my side.

I yelped in surprise and fell to the floor on my face. I slowly got off of the floor and gave my best death glare to an innocent-looking Xavier.

"You jerk!" I yelled throwing a pillow at his.

But him being a stupid alpha werewolf and using his stupid alpha werewolf speed, he dodged the stupid pillow.

"Come on princess. I'm sorry. But it was funny." He smiled up at me.

"Whatever. I'm going to get back at you," I groaned getting up and walking to the door. "I'm going to get a snack. I'll be right back."

"Okay. I'll be waiting," he replied sitting on our bed.

I stopped and turned around.

What better way to get back at him than right now.

"Oh by the way, I called my mom back," I said innocently.

His head shot toward mine. "What did you tell her?"

I smirked. "I told her what happened and she called the cops. They are coming to arrest you right now as we speak."

His face was priceless.

"You aren't leaving me," he growled with glowing gray eyes. I busted out laughing. "Wait. You're kidding, right?"

I gave him another smirk and ran down the stairs screaming.

As I ran through the living room, some of the other wolves in the pack were glancing at me with worried or confused expressions.

"Sam? Are you okay?" Hunter asked me.

"Luna? What's wrong?" an older lady asked me.

"Nothing," I said, watching around me.

"What is going on?" a couple asked, walking to me.

They looked a lot like someone I knew. But I couldn't put my finger on it.

"Well," I said trailing off and rocking back and forth on my feet.

"What did you do?" Hunter asked, giving me a knowing smile.

"For the record, Xavier started it first. I was taking a nap because I was tired and he came into our room and tried to wake me up. But I didn't want to get up so he poked me in my side and I fell on the floor. And I am very ticklish. But anyway, so I decided to get him back. And I told him that I'd told my mom what he'd done, and that the cops were coming to arrest him for kidnapping," I said.

"What happened after that?" the older man asked me with a proud smile.

I didn't know why he was smiling like that, but oh well.

"His wolf got mad and I smiled at him. Then he figured out I was kidding and chased me down the stairs. But I have no idea where he is at," I said looking around.

"You are in a lot of trouble princess," Xavier said grabbing my waist.

"Ah!" I screamed as he picked me up.

"Xavier Cole Slade. Put her down this instant," the older woman said.

Xavier put his head down and lowered me to the floor. "Yes mother."

Whoa, whoa, whoa. Did he just call her his mother?

Oh my gosh.

Xavier's mom was standing in front of me.

She must have been the Luna before I was.

Crap, how did I look?

I wonder if they hate me because I'm human. Shit.

"You must be Sam," she said extending her hand toward me.

"Y-yes Mrs. Slade," I croaked out nervously.

"Please. Call me Tammy." She smiled warmly at me.

"I'm Chris," the older man said shaking my hand.

"Sam," I told him.

"My, my. You are so beautiful," Mrs. —I mean Tammy complimented me.

"Thank you."

So I think Tammy accepted me. That left Chris now. Oh great.

"My wife is right. You are very beautiful. I'm so glad my son has finally found you. You will be a perfect mate for my son, and a damn good Luna." Okay, I had to laugh at that last comment. That was pretty funny. "Especially if you can keep him on his toes with all the joking." He winked.

"Thank you, Chris." I smiled.

"So what is this about kidnapping I hear?" Tammy asked eyeing Xavier.

Another priceless moment. Xavier's face turned white and he froze.

"Uh. No-nothing mother. Come on Sam," Xavier stuttered as he went to grab my hand but I moved it.

"No. Tell them Xavier." I smirked at him.

"Sam," he warned me.

"Nope. Think of this as payback."

He groaned.

"Out with it son," Chris said.

"Okay. WemighthavekidnappedSamandKyrnfromtheirhouse," he rushed out.

"What was that Xavier?" Chris asked.

He opened his mouth but I cut him off.

"Oh nothing. Just how him, Jay, Zander, and Ryan kidnapped me and Kyrn from my house and held us hostage here." I shrugged.

"What?" his parents yelled at the same time.

"At least I got my mate." He let out a nervous laugh and hid behind me.

Like I'm going to stop two full grown werewolves. Get real Xavier. Geez.

His dad sighed and pinched the bridge of his nose. "Could you please tell us what happened, Sam?"

"Sure." I laughed. "Kyrn and I were at home watching sad romance movies because my boyfriend decided to cheat on our two-year anniversary." Xavier growled, but I continued. "I was at a stop lift on my way home crying, when this huge Ford truck pulled up next to me. I looked up and saw Xavier, Jay, Zander, and Ryan. Xavier looked at me and smiled but then got angry. The light changed so I sped off and met Kyrn, who's Jay's mate, at my house.

We were watching a movie when the doorbell rang and I went up to go get it, and there standing on my front porch were the guys. They grabbed me and Kyrn and we both kneed them in their manhood and ran back inside."

Chris laughed. "I can't believe you did that."

"Hey, we were being kidnapped. What else was I supposed to do?" I defended myself, but he only laughed harder. "Well after that, they finally got us pinned to the ground and put chloroform over our mouths and when Kyrn and I woke up, we were both handcuffed to a bed."

I finished telling them the rest of the story, and while Chris looked amused, Tammy looked like she was about to rip off Xavier's head.

"Xavier Cole Slade!" Tammy's voice boomed. Everyone cringed at the sound of her voice. Even Chris. "I did not raise you to treat women like that! You are supposed to love and care for women. Not drug them and kidnap them from their houses!" She screamed and pulled me to her and cradled me. "I raised you to love and cherish women," she said, petting my hair.

I looked over at Chris for some help and he nodded.

"Tammy, dear. She isn't a pet," he said gently grabbing my hand and pulling me from her and toward Xavier.

"Thank you," Xavier said pulling me toward him and wrapping his arms around my waist.

"Look at the bright side, honey," Chris started. "At least he got his mate and we got our Luna—who has some mad driving skills."

Even Tammy let out a small chuckle at that last part.

"I suppose you're right," she said to me and grabbed my hand. "I'm just thankful that you are all right. I am truly sorry you had to find out about us that way."

"It's okay. I'm just glad Xavier and Jay were there before it was too late," I said quietly.

"That is true," Chris added.

"Me too," Xavier said kissing my temple.

"Come. Let's have dinner and learn more about you, Sam," Chris said walking into the dining room.

"I'll start cooking!" Tammy said running to the fridge and pulling out random ingredients.

"Let's go get ready then," Xavier stated, taking my hand and leading us back upstairs. "And don't think I forgot about your little joke. Payback's a bitch." He winked and walking into the bathroom.

Oh crap. I was in some deep shit. Well, better start thinking of something then.

Chapter 19: Dinner Food Fight

Sam

Crap. Right now, I am scared of Xavier's payback. Probably shouldn't have messed with him, but oh well. Can't take it back now.

I grabbed some nicer clothes and ran out of our room. I don't want to be in here when Xavier comes out. Avoiding him will be my best choice right now.

After I ran down some steps and came into another hallway I got lost. I can usually make it downstairs no problem, but I think I took a wrong turn when I was thinking too hard.

I groaned and kept walking forward. A door opened and it turned out to be a bedroom. I quickly shut it. Oops.

"Luna?" a voice said behind me.

I turned around and saw someone from the pack.

"Hi," I smiled nervously at him.

"Are you lost?" he asked.

He looked quite nice. He had shaggy blonde hair, and bright green eyes.

I nodded, embarrassed, and he chuckled.

"Come on," he said with a smile as he motioned for me to follow him. After a five-minute walk, he brought me to the bathroom that is by the living room.

I thanked him and quickly got ready.

After getting ready, I went into the living room to see Xavier, his dad, and some other pack members talking.

Let's not go over there, I thought as I went into the kitchen.

"Hello Mrs.-" She cut me off by giving me a look. "I mean Tammy."

She smiled and nodded.

"Hello dear," she replied warmly.

"Need any help?" I asked.

She gave me a weird look. "You want to help?"

"Sure." I smiled. "I help my mom cook dinner sometimes."

"Oh. Then sure. You can start by cleaning the lettuce if you want," she said as I nodded and headed over to the sink after grabbing the lettuce. "So where are your parents? They are probably freaking with my son kidnapping you. I am deeply sorry about that Sam."

I waved her off. "It's okay. I got a great boyfriend out of it. But she doesn't know. My parents and Kyrn's parents went out of the country to have some adult time for about two months. She doesn't know a thing. But I don't know what I'm going to do when they come back. I highly doubt Xavier will let me leave without him."

"Yes. Ever since we told him about mates, he was always excited about getting one. He told us that she would be beautiful and kind. He was right." She smiled at me and I smiled at her comment. "He loved the idea of having someone made just for him. He also told us that once he got her, he wouldn't let her go and that he would treat her like a princess. He would become protective of his princess. I also know he can be a bit possessive of you."

"A bit?" I asked laughing.

"Okay, okay. Maybe a lot." Tammy giggled.

"There you go." I laughed.

"Is Sam re— Oh, hello Sam," Chris said coming in.

"Hello Chris."

I wondered if they actually accepted me being a human.

What if they just said that because Xavier was right there? What if they think I'm not good enough to be a wolf's mate and a Luna of this pack?

"Are you okay?" Tammy asked me, looking at me concerned.

"Huh? Oh yeah. Uh I'm fine." I tried giving her my best smile but she frowned.

133

"Sweetie. What's wrong?"

"Nothing. It's stupid," I said looking back down at the lettuce.

I heard her put the knife down from when she was cutting the steak. "Sam, you can tell us."

I turned around and saw her and Chris looking at me worriedly.

"Did Xavier do something?" Chris asked. I shook my head. "Then what happened?" he asked softly.

I took a deep breath and looked at them. "Do you guys really accept me?"

Tammy gave me a confused look. "What do you mean?"

I sighed. "Like, do you accept me to become the Luna of this pack?"

"Of course, we do. Why wouldn't we?"

"Well, you know. Because I'm a human and not a werewolf like you guys."

Chris chuckled softly. "Why would it matter of you are human?"

"Because I'm not like you guys. I'm not strong enough, or fast enough, or have heightened senses like you guys have."

"So," Tammy said.

"So, I thought you guys wouldn't accept me," I said looking down.

I heard feet shuffle and the next thing I know Tammy is hugging me.

"Sam. I don't care if you are human. You make my son happy. He's waited for you for a long time and I can't take that away. But I would always accept you. It doesn't matter if you are a human or not. You are my son's mate and our Luna. You are a smart, beautiful, kind, cunning girl," Tammy said softly.

"Everything that Tammy just said is true. You are a part of this family now. The pack already loves you. We love you too," Chris said stepping forward and giving me a hug.

I had tears forming in my eyes. "Thank you," I whispered hugging him back.

I'm so glad they actually accept me.

"And besides. You are quite strong and smart. You took down Ryan, Hunter, and Tim," Chris laughed.

I pulled back and looked at him in shock. How did he know?

"Xavier told us. He thought it was really funny. And you managed to pin him down to the ground for a split second. But it still counts," Chris explained.

"Yeah, about that. Sorry for trying to escape," I apologized.

"Oh don't be sorry. I would have done that too," Tammy said. "Come on. Let's finish getting dinner ready."

The rest of the time we spent getting dinner ready was pretty fun. Tammy and I were cracking jokes about the guys. Chris walked in on us when Tammy said one about him that made me laugh. He huffed and walked right out. Which then in turn caused Tammy and me to laugh even harder.

"Tell us about yourself Sam," Tammy said.

Right now we are at dinner eating steak, mashed potatoes, salad, you name it. It's on the table. I'm eating with Xavier, Tammy, Chris, and a couple other pack members that his parents are close to.

"Okay. Well, umm. I play softball and soccer. I'm an A student, my best friend, practically my sister, is Kyrn. I love animals, ironically my favorite animal is a wolf." Everyone laughed at that. I did a little chuckle myself. "Um, and I want to be a veterinarian."

"You have a bright future ahead of you Sam," Chris said.

"Thank you." I smiled.

"You just keep getting better and better, princess," Xavier stated and gave me a peck on the cheek.

"So I heard the Luna and beta female kicked their guards' asses," John, one of Chris' friends said with a wide smile.

"Oh yes, she did," Xavier said, rubbing his forehead. "I still don't know how she managed to do that. They are two of our best guards and Ryan. And they both took them down."

"I knew I took those classes for a reason." I smiled smugly at him.

He glared at me and stuck his tongue out.

"What classes?" Dr. Tom asked.

I never knew Tom was a good friend of Chris either. They turned out to be best friends from when they were kids.

"My grandfather had talked me into taking self-defense classes. And I didn't want to take then alone, so I dragged Kyrn with me." I laughed. "We took martial arts classes for two and a half years."

"Why did he talk you into it?" Tom asked me.

"I really don't know. He always told me it was because I was a girl and I was going into high school. But I felt like there was a hidden meaning in it."

"Why do you say that?" Chris asked me.

I shrugged. "Every time he told me that, he was so serious. He always said I need to be careful in life and it sounded like it had a double meaning."

"Interesting," Chris said, studying me. Okay so now Chris was confusing me. "How are your grandparents?"

"Actually, it's just my grandfather. My grandmother died in January because of Alzheimer's."

"I'm so sorry," he apologized. He looked at me with such a sorrowful look.

The memories came back, and my eyes were starting to water. "It's okay. You didn't know. But my grandfather is doing well."

"That's good."

"Yeah, it is."

"So Xavier. How was the knee to the manhood?" Chris asked me.

Xavier looked at his dad and glared. "How was the knee to the manhood?" he mocked. "It hurt like hell."

Tammy's mouth fell open and I saw her pick of up a piece of broccoli before she threw it at Xavier's head.

"Watch your mouth, mister," Tammy hissed.

"Mom! Did you just throw food at me?" Xavier asked as he pointed to the piece of broccoli next to his plate.

"Maybe I did. Maybe I didn't," she smiled and looked back down at her food.

But not before Xavier did the worst thing to ever do.

He got a spoonful of mashed potatoes, and flung it at his mom. And it hit her right in the forehead.

"Xavier. Cole. Slade," Tammy got out through clenched teeth.

Xavier leaned back in his chair and crossed his hands behind his head with a smirk plastered on his cute little face. "Yes Mother?"

"Did you just throw food at me?"

"Maybe I did. Maybe I didn't."

Chris cleared his throat. "So Sam, you watch baseball?"

He was trying to change the topic before something got out of hand. But, I have a feeling this fight is far from over between mother and son.

"Yes I do. I'm a Red Sox fan," I said proudly.

"Are you serious? Me too," Chris said.

"No way!" I laughed.

"No one cares about the Red Sox," John said.

"Oh you're just upset because Boston's actually playing in the World Series while the Yankees are sitting at home watching it," I said crossing my arms.

"Ooh. The Luna's got sass," Katie, Tom's wife, said.

John glared at me before stuffing his mouth with steak.

"Yeah. I went there. No one, and I mean no one, disses my team," I said taking a bite of my steak.

This steak is so good!

I heard a smack and felt something wet and small hit my cheek. I wiped it off and saw it was mashed potatoes.

I looked at Xavier and died laughing.

Want to know why? Well, he might have a little, or a lot of mashed potatoes on his face. I saw his mom with a smug expression and had mashed potatoes all over her hand.

"I win," she said smiling at Xavier.

"Oh really?" he asked.

"Really," she countered.

"Oh, shit," Chris said.

With werewolf speed, Xavier grabbed the spoon for the mashed potatoes and flung it at his mom's face.

She gasped and jumped.

"Whoops. Sorry Mother," he said.

"Sam. Can you help me get something in the kitchen?" Chris asked.

"Yeah," I replied jumping out of my chair.

Chris, John, Tom, Katie, and I all jumped out of our chairs and shot into the living room.

When we reached into the living room, we heard a battle cry-like sound and Xavier grunting.

"Luna. Are you guys okay?" someone asked us.

I held up a finger.

"Attention everyone," I said. Everyone immediately stopped talking and looked at me. Oh wow, this is new. So. Much. Attention.

"Okay so, everyone don't pass the living room into the dining room. Or else you will be hit with food." Everyone looked at me like I was crazy. "Don't ask. But it's between Xavier and his mom."

"Want to watch baseball?" Chris asked.

"Yes please." I laughed.

What. A. Night.

Chapter 20: I Don't Like Her

Sam

Last night was… Wow.

After the little food fight Xavier had with his mom, they both came out into the living covered from head to toe in food. Chris and I looked at each before we both fell on the floor laughing. Like literally, we dropped to the floor because we were laughing so hard. It was priceless.

But today it was just me, Kyrn, and Chloe. We had to pick up a cake for Chris' birthday tomorrow. I didn't really know why we were getting it a day early, but Tammy wanted it so we are getting it.

"What was the bakery called again?" Chloe asking while turning onto Main Street.

Kyrn unlocked her phone and looked at the text Tammy sent her. "It's called Sal's Bakery."

"Oh, there it is," Kyrn said as we pulled into a parking spot.

We all got out of the car and headed in.

"Name please?" some lady asked.

"Tammy Slade," Chloe replied.

"Oh yes." She walked into the back and stayed there for a few minutes before she came back out. "It's still cooling. It will be ready in about ten minutes."

"That should be fine. I saw a phone store across the street. I need a new cover for my phone," Kyrn said.

"Okay. Let's go," Chloe stated.

When we walked over, Kyrn headed straight for the galaxy phone section. But while she was over there, I looked for a cover for my Motorola Razor.

"They tell me I'm too young to understand
They say I'm caught up in a dream
Well life will pass me by if I don't open up my eyes
Well that's fine by me"

I looked at my phone and saw my mom calling me.

I let out a laugh as I answered it. "Yes, mom?"

"Hey, honey. How are you?" my mom asked happily.

"The same as when you asked me this morning," I said. She called me twice when I woke up.

"I know. I just miss you," she confessed.

"I miss you too, Mom," I said picking up a red phone cover with black flowers on the right backside.

"Okay so. Um," she started but trailed off.

"Mom? Are you okay? Are you pregnant again?"

"What? No, Sam. We-"

"Oh my gosh! Am I getting a baby sister?" I squeaked excited.

"No!"

"Oh! A baby brother?"

"No. Sam, I'm not pregnant. Your father and I have to stay another week along with Kyrn's parents."

"Oh. How come?" I asked, confused.

Is everything okay?

"Your father got the stomach flu. So we canceled our flight," my mom explained sadly.

"Oh. Is he okay?" I asked concerned.

"Yes dear. He's fine. He's just throwing up a lot."

"Okay."

"I have to go honey. Talk to you later. You father and I miss you and love you."

"Love you too, Mom. Pass it on to dad as well," I said with a sad smile.

"Okay. Bye Sam," my mom replied softly.

"Bye mom," I said and hung up.

"Ready to go?" Chloe asked me.

"Yeah. I'm going to get the red case with the black flowers and swirls," I mumbled as I held the phone case up.

"Sweet. It's cute," she complimented.

I gave her a thankful smile and headed to the cashier person.

"Oh. Look what the cat dragged in," I heard a very high pitched girl voice say behind me.

After the guy handed me my phone case, I turned around and saw none other than Brittany, and I guess one of her friends.

In case you don't remember her, she was the Pizza Hut waitress that continuously lusted over Xavier, Jay, Zander, and Ryan right in front of us.

"Oh boy. Don't you just look adorable?" I lied looking at her booty shorts and low cut top that showed a lot of something that I really didn't want to see.

"Ha ha. Very funny." She glared at me.

I shrugged and put my new cover on my phone. It looked nice.

"Anyway. I hope you guys can come to Pizza Hut again sometime." She smirked as she examined her nails.

"You mean our boyfriends can go to Pizza Hut," Chloe said crossing her arms and glaring.

"Yeah, pretty much."

"Oh honey," Chloe said patting her shoulder. "Hate to break it to you, but they don't like sluts. And besides, they are already taken."

Brittany huffed. "Whatever. They want someone that can take care of their needs. I'm pretty sure you can't make them happy."

Chloe stiffened and started shaking. Her eyes were shifting between black and her normal eye color.

Kyrn and I need to calm her down. And fast.

"Chloe, calm down," Kyrn said trying to soothe her. "Sam. We need to grab the cake and go before she shifts and tears Brittany apart," she whispered the last part to me.

"But I'm pretty sure you're like a walking STD. Like seriously. You need to do homework, not guys," I said, smirking at her shocked expression. "Oh, I'm sorry. Did I insult little miss slut?"

"You...you," she gave me a weak growl and pointed an accusing finger at me.

"Me? Me? What did I do?" I asked tilling my head at her.

"You'll pay for this, you little bitch," she yelled as she stormed out with her friend in tow.

"I really don't like her," I said through gritted teeth.

"Oh, I love my job," the guy said behind us. We all turned to see the guy worker leaning on the counter giving me an amused smile. "Nice come back, by the way."

"Thanks," I smiled laughing as I gave him a bow.

That causes him to laugh even harder.

"Let's get the cake and head over," Kyrn said.

We nodded in agreement and went to go get the cake.

Maybe whatever we don't finish, I can smash into her makeup covered face. Like, come on, she looked like an orange version of an Oompa Loompa from Charlie and Chocolate Factory.

Walking to Sal's Bakery, we grabbed the cake and got in the car. The car ride was pretty silent for a while, but then Chloe decided to break the silence.

"I can't believe she had the nerve to say that to me!" And here we went again.

Chloe has been on this rant thing for like fifteen minutes, starting right when she walked through the door.

"Chloe, honey. You need to calm down. She has nothing on you. You are smart and gorgeous. You have nothing to worry about," Tammy cooed.

We had to ask Tammy for some help because Chloe's wolf was close to taking over.

"I'm not worried about that little orange pumpkin stealing my man. I'm pissed that she had the nerve to say that," she growled out.

"We can always get revenge," I said shrugging.

"Now we're talking," Kyrn said smiling at me.

"What do you mean?" Chloe asked me.

"She works at Pizza Hut, and every restaurant's motto is 'the customer's always right.' Soo-o-o. We just need to do something so stupid her boss will come over and help sort things out, and we can make her look really stupid," I explained.

"I like it," Chloe said with Kyrn and Tammy nodding in agreement.

"You're agreeing to this, Tammy?" I ask in disbelief.

"Of course, Sam. I'm not that strict mom who isn't cool. I can hang and have fun like you teenagers can," she huffed at me.

I laughed. "I'm sorry, but I thought you would object."

"Of course not. She practically drooled over the guys from what you told me and they are taken. I hate it when women do that. It's nasty and so unprofessional. Especially when she was on duty."

"I like you," I said to her.

"Why thank you. I like you too," she said chuckling.

"This is so going to work," Kyrn said determined.

"Sometimes I think you get a little too excited when we are getting revenge on someone," I eyed her.

And what did she do? She rolled her eyes. At me. Little meany.

"Well what do you expect? You come up with great ideas and I enjoy pissing people off when they piss me off." Kyrn scoffed.

I shook my head at her and laughed. "Oh Kyrn. What are we going to do with you?"

"Oh, you know you love me."

"Sadly," Chloe answered for me.

"Jerks!" Kyrn yelled before stomping off into the kitchen. Typical. That girl can eat and eat and eat and not gain any weight. It's amazing.

When we followed her into the kitchen Xavier and Zander came in.

"Hey babe," Xavier said walking up to me and giving me a kiss on the cheek.

"Hey," I replied and took a seat at the table.

"Where's Jay?" Kyrn asked looking around.

"Patrol," he answered.

"Ah. Okay."

"Guess what tomorrow is?" Xavier asked excited all of the sudden.

"Uh, your dad's birthday?"

"Yes. But that's not what I'm talking about."

"Then what?"

"Your first day of training starts tomorrow," he exclaimed clapping.

Ah shit.

"You're kidding, right?" I said groaning.

"Nope," he stated, popping the 'p'. I groaned and rested my head against the table. I felt him rub my back and chuckle. "But it will be okay because both Jay and I are taking tomorrow off from pack duties, and we are being your guys' personal trainers."

"Why not someone else? You guys don't have to take time off."

"We know. But we both talked it over and we don't any guys touching what is ours." His tone went from joyful to dead serious in a matter of seconds.

"Aw. Is someone not happy?" I teased with a smirk.

He stuck his tongue out at me. "No. I just don't want any guys touching you."

"I'll be fine," I stated trying to relax him.

"I don't care. I don't want anyone else training you and that's final." With that he headed upstairs, probably to take a shower or something.

"Well, then," I said dramatically.

"That's my son for you," Tammy joined in.

"He seems cranky. I'm going to go check on him," I said before heading up the stairs.

When I got to our room, I he was lying down on the bed with his hands over his face. I walked over and sat on the edge of the bed.

"I'm sorry," he apologized.

"No, I'm sorry. I shouldn't have made a big deal out of it," I cut him off.

"No, not that." He rolled over and faced me.

"Then what?" I asked confused.

"I'm sorry for being cranky."

"Xavier, its fine. I shouldn't have said that stuff."

He shook his head at me. "No. My wolf is still irritated."

"About what?"

"Brett and Trey. He's mad because they're both still alive."

"Well, he doesn't need to kill them."

"Well he wants to," he confessed pulling me onto his lap.

"He's not going to kill them," I demanded, crossing my arms.

"Try telling him that," Xavier said playing with my fingers.

"Fine. I will."

His head snapped to mine. "Are you sure."

"Yes. I don't want him thinking he can just go around killing whoever hurts me," Xavier growled and I slapped his chest playfully. "Let me talk to him."

"Okay. If you want to," he said before closing his eyes.

After a few more minutes, he reopened then and I saw glowing stormy gray eyes.

"Yes, princess?" Ryder asked me burying his face in my neck and sniffing.

I shivered, and felt him smirk.

Stupid mate pull-thingy.

"You do realize that you can't go kill Brett and Trey, right?"

His head snapped up and I heard a slight crack. "And why not?" he growled. "They deserve it and much worse!"

"Just because he punched me by accident doesn't mean you can go around killing him," I stated, standing up.

He stood up too and walked over to me. "If I had my way, he would be begging for me to end his pathetic little life."

"Well you can't." I crossed my arms over my chest and he raised his eyebrows at me before doing the same thing.

"And why not?"

"Because I said so."

"Princess. I'm the alpha."

"And I'm the alpha female. Aren't I?" I questioned. He looked at me in shock before glaring at me. That's what I thought. He growled softly at me and I smirked. "And we are equal. Aren't we?"

He growled again, before reluctantly nodding, but still glaring. "But still."

"No buts. You aren't killing them."

"I could if I wanted to," he shot back.

"Not if you want an angry mate to deal with."

"Don't you pull the mate card with me, princess."

I smiled innocently. "I don't know what you are talking about."

"You know damn well what I'm talking about."

I tapped my chin pretending to think. "Nope. Doesn't ring a bell."

He walked up to me and pulled me into his chest. "You are so lucky you're my mate."

"Why?" I asked him hugging him back.

"Because I would have to punish you for talking to me like that. But then again," he trailed off pulling away from me slightly. "I could still punish you. But in a different way." He winked at me before kissing my mark.

"Ryder," I said softly.

"Hm?" He asked, still sucking on my mark.

"Bad dog," I giggled pushing him off me.

"Hey. That's offensive." Ryder said sternly, trying to hide a smile.

I grinned and shrugged.

He closed his eyes and they were back to normal.

"Let's go back downstairs," I said tugging on his hand.

Men and their horny wolves. What are you going to do with them?

Chapter 21: Plan Is In Action

Sam

It'd been a day since our little run in with Brittany and her slut crew.

And today, we were going to order a pizza from Pizza Hut and go pick it up. But! We may or may not order a wrong pizza and tell her we didn't order it when we get there. But of course, we had to wait until after training to do that. And I wasn't looking forward to the training one bit.

A couple of reasons. One, it was freaking five in the morning; two, Xavier will be my trainer; and three, he trains shirtless. Shirtless! I'm not going be able to concentrate on anything—he has an extremely fine body and an amazing eight-pack. So tell me if you could avoid looking at that. Yeah, I didn't think so.

"Ready to get up, babe?" Xavier asked from beside me.

"Hell to the no," I mumbled with my face in the pillow.

"Come on. We have to get ready for your training session."

"Oh, freaking bite me!" I spat out pushing him away softly and pulling a pillow over my head.

I heard him chuckle.

"Your wish is my command," I heard Xavier growl.

I felt the pillow being moved off my head, and his body moved on top of mine preventing me from moving. He held my wrists in his hand and placed feathery kisses around my mark.

Shit. What did I get myself into?

"Xa-Xavier," I stuttered out.

"Yes, princess?" he asked before going back to kissing my mark.

"I-I was kidding," I said clenching my fists to keep from moaning out.

"I wasn't."

I felt his teeth become pointier and knew he was actually dead serious. I tried to wiggle out of his hold, but I felt his little mini me come join us on my butt and he groaned.

"Stop. Moving," he said.

I let out a nervous giggle, while he let out a low possessive growl.

"Mine," he said softly. "You're all mine."

Okay so that time, I did let out a moan. Not my smartest idea, but hey I couldn't help it, okay?

"Who's that?" I shouted looking to my left.

Xavier jumped off me going into a defensive stance and growling.

"Where?" He asked, scanning the room.

But I had already got up, grabbed the clothes I laid out last night, and run into the bathroom locking the door.

"No one," I laughed.

"What the hell?" he roared, slamming his fists down on the bathroom door.

"I needed a shower, but you were too busy attacking my neck."

"Well, sorry for wanting to kiss my girlfriend."

"You are such a dork." I laughed out getting in the shower.

"Wait!" he suddenly yelled out.

"What?"

"Can I take one with you? We could save water."

"Ha ha! No!" I yelled back laughing.

You wouldn't want to take a shower. Maybe something else I will not name.

"Fine, hurry up then. I have to take a cold shower," he mumbled the last part.

I busted out laughing. I was laughing so hard I had to hold onto the wall to avoid slipping and possibly hurting myself.

"Yeah, yeah. Laugh it up," Xavier grumbled.

"Oh gosh. That's gold," I said wiping away tears.

Finally got ready and headed downstairs to the front door. Xavier was telling me everything I would be doing today as we walked to the training field.

"Why can't I use my sais?" I asked annoyed.

"Because you are supposed to be using your fists. And no more using sias. If you are going to use a weapon, it's either daggers or bows n' arrows," Xavier said all teacher-like.

"Why?"

"Daggers are small and lightweight. Same with bows n' arrows, except for the small part. But you can have a carrier go across your back for your arrows, and you can sling the bow over your shoulder."

"Fine," I muttered charging at him.

He quickly side-stepped me and tripped me with his foot causing me to roll across the dirt.

I groaned and slammed my fist on the ground and stood up. I wiped the dirt from my face and glared at his smirking face.

"You don't have very good balance do you?"

I clenched my fist and my body started shaking. He is pissing me off so much right now.

"Awe what's wrong baby? Are you getting upset?"

I shut my eyes tight and tried breathing in and out slowly.

Calm down. Stay calm Sam. Stay calm. Just ca—.

"Well I guess you *are* a girl, so this is expected of you," Xavier said. I could hear the smirk in his voice.

My eyes snapped open and I launched my body forward and tackled him to the ground. We started rolling, and I stopped so I was straddling him and I was hitting him.

"You. Stupid. Little. Jerk," I screamed out with each hit.

"Ah! Sam!" Xavier yelled trying to block all my hits.

He finally got hold of my wrists and rolled us over so he was on top.

"Shit babe. Your hits hurt." Xavier laughed.

I was struggling to get back on top and hit him some more, but maddeningly he had pinned my wrists above my head.

"You little jerk face," I growled.

"That's not very nice to say, princess. Oh and by the way. I love this position." He wiggled his eyebrows and leaned down so he was only inches from my face.

"Why did you say all that stuff? To get under my skin?"

"Yes pretty much. I've noticed that you do a very good job when you are upset. And to be honest, you look pretty sexy when you are mad."

"Oh really?" I smirked, leaning up toward his face.

"Really," he said before he connected our lips.

After a few seconds, he loosened his grip on my wrists. I used that as the perfect opportunity to get my feet under him, and flipped him over.

"Oof," he let out, landing on his back.

I got up and flipped him over so quickly he was shocked. I pulled out the handcuffs I had hidden, put his hands behind his back and handcuffed them before standing up.

"There we go." I admired my work.

"Hey! Sam! What the hell?" Xavier asked sitting up.

"I'm done with training for today. See you tomorrow," I called out walking away.

"You are so dead when I get out of here!"

I turned around and gave him a sweet smile. "Ha! Good luck getting out when you don't have the key."

He growled loudly and a shiver racked through my spine. He smirked and looked at me with a creepy grin.

I'm kind of scared right now. Is that bad?

"Yeah. But I also have a mate that is extremely ticklish. And my wolf wants to do some things to. Like have you all to himself," he trailed off making me gulp loudly and his eyes turn black with lust. "He wants to—"

"Don't need to know!" I screamed and covered my ears.

151

He laughed and looked at me again with he calmed down. "Okay, now seriously, unlock these."

"Nope!" I yelled and ran into the house laughing like a hyena.

All I could think about was how much shit I would be in when he gets out.

"Ready to go pick up the pizza?" Chloe asked Kyrn and me.

"Yes ma'am." I saluted.

We ordered our pizza and we got garlic, sausage, pepperoni, onions, peppers, and then the other half cheese.

About thirty minutes later, we arrived at Pizza Hut and we saw Brittany at the delivery section.

"Name please?" she asked not paying attention to who we were.

"Slade," I answered.

"Oh yes of course. Your pizza is ri—oh it's you," she said placing the pizza down on the counter and crossing her arms. Wow, attitude much?

"Hey Brittany. You are looking as lovely as ever," I said smiling at her.

"Whatever. It'll be $15.87." Oh, the attitude was still there.

"Here you go. Keep the change," Chloe said handing her a twenty-dollar bill.

"Wow. Thanks." Brittany rolled her eyes and ignored us by turning around and talking to another worker.

"Shall we go?" I asked walking out with Chloe and Kyrn in tow.

"Wait. What about our revenge?" Kyrn asked speaking up.

"We have to wait a little bit, and then when we check it, we go back in," I explained opening it up then closing and walking back in.

I winked at the girls and they giggled.

"How can I help you?" Brittany asked, typing on the computer.

"Yes. This isn't the pizza we ordered," I explained calmly.

"Oh I'm so sorry," she apologized looking up. "Oh. What now?" She yelled in a whispered so no one would hear her.

I smirked and set the pizza on the counter. "We didn't order this pizza."

"Yes you did," she replied in a duh tone.

"No. We ordered half cheese and half sausage."

"No. You had half cheese and half sausage, peppers, onions, pepperoni, and garlic."

"No."

"Yes."

"No."

"Yes!"

"No!"

"Yes!"

"What is going on in here?" a man asked walking in.

I looked at his nametag and it had the word manager on it. Score!

"She mixed up our order and she is trying to tell us we ordered what we got," Kyrn yelled from behind me.

"No! You guys called in that order!" Brittany yelled at us.

"Whoa, whoa, whoa. Okay, miss please tell me what happened." He gestured to us.

"Well," Chloe started. "We ordered half cheese and half sausage. But instead she gave us half cheese and half sausage, pepperoni, peppers, onions, and garlic."

"That's because you ordered that!"

"Brittany! We do not yell at customers," he scolded her. She looked down and nodded her head. "Good. Now go make them the pizza they originally ordered and give them a refund," he ordered.

"Yes sir," she mumbled and trotted off to the oven.

"My apologies, ladies. I'm so sorry your order got mixed up," the manager rushed out.

"It's okay. We all make mistakes," I reassured him with a big smile.

We waited for another twenty minutes until the pizza was ready and Brittany called us up.

"Here's your pizza," she spat out.

"Aw, thank you dear," Chloe said laughing and grabbed the pizza and the twenty that we gave Brittany earlier.

"You guys set me up. Didn't you?" Brittany accused us.

"You know us so well." I winked and walked out after I saw her shocked face.

Life is so good.

Chapter 22: Paybacks A Bitch

Sam

"Did you see her face?" Kyrn asked us laughing as we got out of the car.

"It was priceless!" I said while Chloe nodded in agreement.

"Oh, wow. I love pissing people off."

"We know," Chloe and I said simultaneously.

Kyrn huffed and crossed her arms over her chest. "Well then."

We all got a kick out of that and continued walking.

Once we got the kitchen, we put the pizza down and noticed the house seemed empty.

"Where are the guys?" Chloe asked.

Kyrn and I shrugged and we turned around and froze at the sight.

There were the guys. Standing there with the whipped cream in the spray bottle thing.

"Payback a bitch, huh princess?" Xavier said smirking as he zeroed in on me.

"Is this because you handcuffed him during training this morning?" Chloe asked me completely annoyed at the outcome.

"Yes. Yes it is," Xavier answered for me.

"Then why are Zander and Jay holding whipped cream also?" Chloe asked as she pointed to them.

"We thought it would be fun," Jay said smirking at Kyrn.

"Did I ever tell you how sexy you look in that white V-neck babe?" I asked trying to get Xavier's mind off of shooting me with whipped cream.

I saw his eyes darken and start to turn to that glowing, stormy gray color. I smirked, knowing it was working. So I decided to keep going.

"I mean your muscles really pop out. It's looks re-e-eally nice on you. Then there's your abs. And the V-neck doesn't really hide them at all." I winked.

Ever since that day when Xavier asked me to be his girlfriend, I've been a lot more comfortable around him. I've gotten bolder and more self-confident with him around me all the time. I feel like I can really be myself, and I don't have to worry about him judging me.

His eyes turned to pitch black with lust and he stepped toward me.

But sadly he seemed to see what I was doing, and shook his head letting out a frustrated growl.

"Dammit," he mumbled while the guys laughed at him. "Hey! It's not my fault. My wolf is a freaking horn dog."

"Well, what I'm saying is true." I smiled sweetly at him.

He smiled but replaced it with a scowl.

"Sam," he groaned.

I giggled and he gave me a warm smile. "Yes?"

"You're still not getting out of your payback."

"But why—" I stopped when he pushed down the nozzle and whipped cream flew at my face. "Xavier!" I screamed.

"Yes, princess?" he asked holding his stomach from laughing so hard.

"Come here." I opened my arms out wide for him and he gave me the are-you-crazy look. "Please?"

"Sorry babe, but no."

"Oh, wow. Xavier just said no to his little princess," Jay snickered.

"Yeah and it was hard." He turned and gave me a smile, then leaned down to whisper in his ear. But I heard all of it. "That's probably the only time I will ever say no to her."

Good to know.

While he wasn't facing me, I ran up to him and jumped on his back and rubbed my face and hands on him to get the whipped cream off.

"Hey!" He yelled.

I jumped off laughing. "Got ya."

"This is my favorite V-neck," he mumbled trying to get the whipped cream off.

"Payback's a bitch, huh?" I mocked him using his own words.

"Touché my beautiful mate. Touché. But, you should probably run, little one."

I squeaked and booked it up the stairs toward our bathroom. Not even two seconds later, I heard Xavier's boots making noise as he hauled up the stairs after me. I got to the bathroom door and locked it.

He pounded on the door and growled. "You are so lucky princess. Okay, I'm going to go clean up, and then I'll be back."

I breathed a sigh of relief and turned on the water, listening to his footsteps leave the room.

I waited for a few moments remembering I didn't grab any clothes. Once I knew the coast was clear, I ran out and grabbed clothes and ran back in the bathroom as fast as I could. I didn't want to take any chances, with him being an alpha after all.

After my shower, I walked into the bedroom to see him sitting on the bed staring and smiling at me.

"Hi," he said all cheery like.

"Hi?" I said back slightly confused.

"Get all cleaned up?"

"Yeah. Didn't take that long."

"I could have just licked you clean," he suggested like it was nothing.

"Xavier!"

"Sorry," he laughed. "My wolf is, like, freaking out."

"Why? Is he okay?" I wondered all of the sudden as I ran over to him.

"Yeah he's fine. He's just been really horny lately. Ever since I marked you, he's been wanting to claim you. He doesn't like the idea of you wandering around unmated with a bunch of unmated male wolves around. And, well, neither do I," Xavier admitted.

Aw! He looked so cute. His face was slightly red and he was looking down at my hands as he played with my fingers.

"Oh Xavier," I said and gave him a kiss.

He smiled instantly and returned the kiss by wrapping his arms around my waist and pulled me into his lap. He pulled away and gave me a huge grin.

"I'm glad I have you as a mate. I wouldn't trade you for anything in the world." He gave me a quick peck and pulled away again. "Oh. The guys and I were wondering if you girls wanted to go out for a movie or something."

"Sure. What movie?" I felt excited all of the sudden.

"Oh. Um…I don't know. We were going to have you girls pick the movie." He shrugged.

"Okay, let's go!" I yelled and grabbed his hand before sprinting down the stairs.

"What's this about a movie Zander is talking about?" Chloe asked walking into the living room.

"The guys wanted to know if we wanted to go watch a movie. And we get to pick the movie," I told her.

"What movie?" Kyrn asked.

"Girls. Huddle up!" I shouted as we all ran into the kitchen and got in a circle.

"Okay, let's go over this," I told them.

"No scary movie. Even though I hate them, it's better to watch them at night," Chloe explained while I nodded.

"Sounds good. Let's make them watch something they won't enjoy. Payback for getting whipped cream on all of us," Kyrn's idea was pretty good.

"Okay. Something that's 3D. 3D is a must," I added on.

"So far so good," Kyrn smiled.

"I know! One Direction: This Is Us," Chloe said.

158

"Perfect!" Kyrn and I squealed in excitement.

Chapter 23: Bad News

Sam

I'm finally nineteen. Oh, wow I feel old.

I remember junior high like it was yesterday. Oh gosh. Ms. Luft hated Kyrn and me.

We always talked too much and I remember she was terrified of snakes, and on April fool's day, we got my pet snake Sammy and put her in Ms. Luft's desk.

Let's just say, we got two weeks' detention. But it was totally worth it. Her facial expression was priceless. Oh, good times, good times.

I was snapped out of it when I heard my phone going off.

"Hey mom," I said smiling when I answered it.

"Hey dear. How are you?"

"I'm good. You?"

"We are pretty good. And guess what?" She squealed with excitement.

"What?" I laughed.

"We are coming home tomorrow! Isn't that exciting?"

Oh no.

I dropped the phone out of shock but quickly went to go pick it up. "Yeah. That's wonderful Mom. Why so early though?"

"Well your dad is feeling a whole lot better and so we decided to come home early. We miss you girls."

"We miss you too, Mom," I whispered.

I couldn't believe this was happening.

"Sorry we can't be home on your actual birthday. But we will be home bright and early tomorrow morning for you. We are going to give you a late birthday party."

"Gee. Thanks mom," I said trying to sound convincing.

"I know. Isn't it great?" My mom asked excited.

"Yeah. Totally," I replied.

"I know. Well we have to go. I love you."

"Love you too, Mom," I told her hanging up before running down the stairs.

I ran into the kitchen and saw the gang there— Xavier, Jay, Zander, Hunter, Tim, Kyrn, and Chloe.

"Whoa, babe. You okay?" Xavier asked walking up to me.

I shook my head and turned to Kyrn. "They are coming home tomorrow."

She spat out her water and looked at me horrified. "What did you just say?"

"They. Are. Coming. Home. Tomorrow. Morning."

"No way. Are you serious?" Kyrn asked, worried.

"Yeah. She just called me."

"Who's coming home tomorrow?" Jay asked looking to and fro between Kyrn and me.

"Our parents," Kyrn and I said.

"Oh, shit," Xavier mumbled, running a hand down his face.

"What are we going to do?"

"I don't know," Kyrn said hitting her head on Jay's shoulder.

He grabbed her head and kissed her forehead.

"We have to go back home," I said.

"No!" Xavier growled.

"Why not?" I asked him.

"Mine," he growled again and pulled me to his chest.

"Xavier. I can't stay here tonight. They are coming bright and early because they are upset about missing my birthday."

"But. No, you can't leave," Xavier whined.

"Well, guess what? Kyrn and I have to leave tonight."

"No!" Jay growled.

"Jay—" Kyrn started, but he shook his head, not listening to us.

"You are mine. So you are staying here," Jay said sternly.

"You are so stubborn," she said shaking her head.

"Yes I am, and I'm proud of it."

"Men are so stupid," Chloe stated.

"So are women," Hunter defended.

"But women are far more superior," Chloe smirked.

"Yeah right."

"You want to bet?" Chloe challenged.

"Sure," Hunter said accepting the challenge.

"Okay. Close your eyes."

"How will this prove anything?" He asked.

"Trust me."

"Why?"

"Just do it Hunter," Chloe whined.

He sighed but nodded and closed his eyes. Chloe gave us a sly smile and snecked to the fridge.

She quietly opened it and pulled out a pie that Xavier's mom had made me for my birthday.

She walked over to Hunter still holding it. "Okay. Open your eyes."

Once he opened his eyes, she took it and smashed it into his face.

"Ah!" He jumped while the rest of us were laughing. "How does this prove anything?" Hunter yelled at Chloe.

"It shows that men will so anything women say." She smiled.

"She got ya there, man." Tim laughed.

"Oh shut it." Hunter chuckled before walking up the stairs—probably to a shower.

"That was my birthday pie," I whispered as I walked over to the mess. "You killed him," I fake cried dramatically.

"Oh honey. We will get you a new and better pie," Xavier cooed wrapping his arms around me.

"He was so young. Just waiting to be eaten. It was his dream. But now he will never have a chance to fulfill his dream because Chloe ruined it!" I accused pointing a figure at her.

"Oh, boo hoo," she teased.

I let out a warrior cry as I picked up some of the pie and smashed it in her face.

"You got a little something in your face," I teased back and she gasped at me.

"You little meany," she laughed.

The next thing I knew, she pulled me in for a hug and rubbed her face all over me.

"Thanks a lot. Now I need to go take a shower."

"I'll join you. You know, because I'm all about saving water and helping the environment," Xavier smiled walking up to me.

"You can help the environment by having your wolf poop on the ground. His poop can be used as fertilizer." I smiled smugly at his shocked face.

"Rejected!" Jay and Zander shouted.

They gave each other a high five and Xavier huffed.

"Fine," he mumbled and licked my cheek before running into the living room.

"Sicko!" I shouted laughing.

I walked up the stairs and into the bathroom before grabbing clothes to wear. I wonder what I'm going to do about my mom and dad coming back.

***

Xavier

"Is everything set for tonight?" I asked.

After Sam walked up the stairs to take her shower when Chloe got pie all over her face, I decided we should start discussing the plans for tonight.

163

"Yep. We get your dad's sailboat ready and set up, and all you have to do is get the food. We've got the table, chairs, and candlesticks along with the cups and silverware," Chloe said, looking through her phone where she recorded everything.

"Okay. Sounds good."

"What drinks are you going to have?" Kyrn asked.

"I was thinking some fancy wine?" She nodded approvingly.

"Okay. Now food," I said as I looked at Kyrn.

"Well she loves sea food," Kyrn said. "Crab, lobster, shrimp, and catfish are her favorite."

"Okay. Now we've just got to put that all together," Chloe said.

"We could have shrimp and crab as an appetizer, then catfish with a side of lobster as an entree. Then for dessert, I know she loves mint chocolate chip ice cream."

"Perfect. I have it all set," Chloe said waving her phone.

"Excellent." I smiled. "Thanks."

"No problem."

"Why aren't you ever this romantic?" Kyrn asked Jay.

"Uh. Well I…" he started, but trailed off, not knowing where he was going with this.

"Exactly," she huffed.

'Help', Jay asked through the mind link.

'Well, when is her birthday?' I asked.

'November eleventh,' Jay said.

'We'll do something like this for your one-month anniversary.'

He looked up at me with a huge smile. 'Awesome. Thanks dude. I owe you.'

I laughed. 'Nah it's cool. We can tell them you planned it. I owe you for helping with this surprise birthday date.'

'I think we're even.'

'Deal.'

"What are you guys talking about?" I jumped when I heard Sam's sweet voice pop out of nowhere.

164

"Nothing, princess. Just about how Hunter got his ass handed to him by Chloe," I smiled and pecked her cheek.

"That is pretty funny." She smiled.

"Of course. Because everything that happens to Hunter is funny," Hunter complained.

"Come on, man," I said. "It's pretty funny."

"Gee, thanks alpha." He stuck his tongue out at me.

I smiled back at him and he rolled his eyes.

"We can get Xavier next time, Hunter," Sam said.

"I like that idea Sam."

"I'm in," Chloe said.

"Me too," Jay and Kyrn put their hands in.

"I hate all of you," I teased, laughing.

"We love you too," Sam pecked my lips.

"I love you," I said against her lips.

"I love me too." She smiled. I gave her a look and she smiled up at me. "I love you too."

"Good," I said pulling her into a hug. "Now let's get you to your house."

***

Sam

The drive to my house was pretty quiet. Xavier was deep in thought and everyone was pretty much just very quiet. I really don't know what was going on in everyone's heads. But we finally made it.

"Remember to call me every thirty minutes. And remember, if you ever feel lonely, just call me. Oh and don't worry about being scared, I'm having at least twenty wolves patrol your house twenty-four seven." And Xavier kept going on and on as Jay went with Kyrn up to our guest room to drop her bags off.

So here we are standing in my living room, and I have twenty wolves, which are on the first shift in my house. Yeah, he wasn't kidding.

I cut off his rant with a kiss on the lips. He responded immediately and deepened the kiss.

A low growl vibrated through his chest and I had to pull away before things got too heated.

"Xavier," I laughed as he closed his eyes resting his forehead against mine. "Stay calm. I'll be fine. I have at least twenty wolves patrolling my house like you said. So stop worrying okay?"

He sighed, but reluctantly nodded. "Okay. I'm sorry. I'm just, just really worried. I'm leaving you alone."

"I'm not alone, remember?" I teased pointing to the twenty warrior wolves standing in my living room.

They looked over and smiled.

"I know." He gave me one last kiss. "I have to go to a meeting, but I will call you when I'm done. So you better be by your phone every second. Because even if you miss one call or text, I'm coming over no matter what." "

"Yes, alpha," I teased and stuck my tongue out.

He growled and pulled me closer. "It's so sexy to hear you call me that princess."

I shivered but snapped out of it.,I pushed his shoulder lightly. "Get going before you're late, horn dog."

He smirked and pecked my lips one more time.

"Only for you. Love you," he said.

"Love you," I called out to him.

He smiled and walked out. But not before barking orders at the other wolves.

"You guys hungry?" I asked them.

They stopped what they were doing and nodded frantically. I laughed and they came running into the kitchen, sitting at the island and table.

After I cooked for them and listened to Xavier all night, I got dressed in my bathroom and walked over to my window seat and sat down.

It's the first night in two months that I'll be sleeping by myself. I'm going to admit it feels kind of lonely without him.

But I'm also excited to see my parents. I missed them so much. Kyrn's in the same position. Jay had warrior wolves patrol for her as well. We were joking about it before we both went to bed.

I laughed to myself at how our mates are. But that's what I love about Xavier. He's overprotective, possessive, stupid, and childish. But that's who he is.

I looked at the moon and smiled. Every time I see the moon, I think about Xavier. I opened my window and leaned against the window sill. I was about to close it, but I heard a howl. It sounded so familiar. It sent chills down my spine and I looked down to see Hunter making kissy faces at me.

Then it clicked. It was Xavier.

"Oh shut up!" I shouted playfully at him. The wolves laughed and smiled at me. "Goodnight guys."

All the wolves stopped moving and looked at me. "Night, Luna," they shouted before looking serious again and walking around.

Printed in Great Britain
by Amazon

54644616R00104